OUTFOXED BY MURDER

An Amy Bell Mystery

DAVID SCHWINGER

Copyright © 2024 David Schwinger
All rights reserved
First Edition

PAGE PUBLISHING
Conneaut Lake, PA

First originally published by Page Publishing 2024

Although some named locations, such as City College, are real, all depictions of persons, events, and policies at any and all locations in this book are intended to be completely fictional.

ISBN 979-8-89315-895-3 (pbk)
ISBN 979-8-89315-911-0 (digital)

Printed in the United States of America

Also by David Schwinger

The Teacher's Pet Murders
Murder Spoils the Perfect Romance
Murder with Magic
Murder Takes the Top Prize
Murder on the Lido Deck
Letter-Perfect Murder
Willing to Murder
Retirement Was Murder
Reputation for Murder
Murder Couldn't Wait
Murder Makes Music
Murder Hits the Campaign Trail
Murder Saves the Day
Murder Finds a Way
Murder in Reverse
Murder Was Necessary

To all the wonderful members of our community's Travel Club who have joined us on trips that Sherryl and I have led. Looking forward to more adventures ahead!

Saturday, September 22, 2018

Having read the invitation that had just arrived in the mail, Bill Santori laughed and bellowed out, "The Fox! Wow, the return of the Fox!"

Jean Santori put the TV on pause and came into the kitchen from the living room to join her husband. "Honey, did you say, 'the Fox'? What are you referring to?"

He smiled. "Yeah, that was the nickname Lance Redding gave himself, starting when we were both juniors at Balch College."

"Where is Balch College again? I know you mentioned it a few times, when we were dating, as being a small private college, but you mainly spoke about NYU Law School."

"Balch College is in Valley Stream, Long Island, and it was named after Roland Balch, a real estate developer in the area. I think the majority of Balch students—at least in my graduating class—were from Queens. You're right, I rarely mentioned it, but I didn't have too much time, given our whirlwind romance and marriage. Can you believe we first met only fourteen months ago?"

Jean smiled and nodded. She gave her husband a passionate, prolonged kiss, and then he continued.

"Anyhow, Balch College had sports teams that competed against those of other small colleges. We had baseball and basketball teams, with both of them using the nickname the 'Foxes.' Sometimes, they called themselves the 'Fabulous Foxes.' But they didn't make a big thing about it, other than encouraging fans at their games to shout out, 'Go, Foxes, go Foxes!'

"But that changed during our junior year. Lance unilaterally decided to be the mascot for the two sports teams. He acquired a full-body fox costume, including a 'smiling' fox head. Then he went to one of their basketball games and danced around, before the game and at halftime, leading audience chants of 'Go, Foxes!'

"Suddenly, Lance became a big celebrity, and he became a sort of PR representative for the college as well as for the sports teams. He even sometimes wore his fox costume to class.

"And Lance also became a magnet for many women students. I have no first-hand knowledge, but the story around the school was that he had gone out with well over a dozen women."

"Honey," his wife interrupted, "after Lance graduated, what happened? Did another student become the new fox?"

He shook his head. "Nobody took over in the fox outfit. But Lance still made some appearances at Balch College events, wearing his costume. I think he still does that now, more than ten years after we graduated. And, even now, Lance often refers to himself as 'the Fox,' or 'the Fabulous Fox.' I guess he still gets a big kick out of the whole thing."

"Honey, did Lance get married?"

"Yeah, twice, and he got divorced twice, both times after less than a year. But he parlayed his fame and popularity into a high-paying job at a consulting firm. I think his main role there has been to attract clients.

"Once—or sometimes twice—a year, he throws a big 'fox party' at his home in Great Neck. Massive buffet, live music and other entertainment, and a stand-up comedy performance by Lance, who wears his fox costume for the whole event. He generally has a different group of invited guests at each party, although he also has a few 'regulars.'

"And now, I just received this invitation—my first ever—to his fox party, scheduled for Saturday, October 6, from 5:00 to 9:00 p.m. He invited every member of the Balch College weekly political discussion group during our senior year. Of course, Lance was a member, and so was I. Each invitee can bring one additional guest. I want to go; are you interested?"

She shook her head. "Not really. Unless it's important to you that I go, I'll pass. Maybe I'll spend that weekend with my sister and her family. I haven't seen them in a while."

Bill smiled, nodded, and kissed his wife. "No problem; I'll reconnect at the party with some fellow Balch students that I haven't seen in a decade. But you probably would not know any of them. So have a good time at your sister's."

"Honey, thanks for understanding. I'll bet you're really looking forward to seeing Lance again, in his fox costume, doing his thing."

He laughed. "You bet!"

Sunday, September 23, 2018

Marilyn Waller answered her phone and immediately realized that Doris Mays, the person who had called, was quite agitated.

"Hi, Marilyn, this is Doris. Guess who just invited me to a big party that he's throwing at his home!"

Marilyn laughed. "I have no idea, but I'll make an educated guess: Mike Pence."

"Ha-ha, very funny. I'll give you a hint: when he and I were seniors and in a political discussion group at Balch College, he nearly raped me."

"Oh, my god, Doris, do you mean Lance Redding?"

"Yep, the Fox. So you do remember when I originally told you what he did, right? And Lance never admitted that he did anything wrong; in fact, I doubt that he even remembered what happened. He just went on to another woman. Isn't that special?"

"So are you gonna go to his party and remind him? He certainly deserves to have the whole thing thrown back into his face."

"I'm thinking yes, and I can bring a guest. Are you interested? It's Saturday, October 6, from 5 to 9 in the evening. There'll be lots of entertainment, including Lance, dressed in his fox suit. He lives in Great Neck. I'll take you there and back in my car."

"Sure, Doris, but you have to promise me that you will not make a big scene. It's not worth it. You can speak to him privately at the party."

"Okay, Marilyn, I promise, even though I remember hearing some gossip, at that time, about Lance mistreating other girls. By the way, did Lance ever come on to you?"

"Believe it or not, if I didn't have a boyfriend back then—you remember Steve—I might have actually come on to Lance! Once he became known as the Fox, he was strangely alluring! But to answer your question, Lance never came on to me. Hey, maybe I can come on to some great guy at Lance's party—or, hopefully, vice versa. I've reached the point where I would like to be married. How about you?"

Doris laughed. "Me too, Marilyn, me too!"

Monday, September 24, 2018

"Hey, Ralph, it's good to hear from you; it's been a few years. How are things going?" Howard Argus used to talk with his college buddy Ralph Kane more frequently, but as is so often the case, time and increasing obligations had taken their toll. Over the past few years, he had left a few text and voicemail messages for Ralph, but they had not been returned. So this phone call from Ralph was a welcome surprise.

"Hectic business situation, Howie, but no complaints, really. I'm embarrassed that I have not returned your messages. Well, in any case, now we have a chance to get together, at a big fox party! I assume you got Lance's invitation, and you'll be going, right?"

"Ralph, if you're definitely going, then I'll go too. But before you called, I was not planning to attend. Lance was quite the scumbag. I don't think I ever told you about this, but for about a month, when we all were seniors and in the discussion group—just before I graduated one semester early, in January—I had a girlfriend, Joan. Lance knew about this, and, regardless, he enticed Joan to dump me and go with him. Then as soon as he got Joan to have sex with him—which took a while, because Joan was an old-fashioned, religious girl—he dumped her. Actually, they had one more date, where they went back to his apartment, and he found some ridiculous pretext to push her up against a wall and say, 'I'm done with you; get out of here!' Then he dragged her out the door."

"Good grief, Howie, that's awful!"

"I know all this because Joan filled me in on those details when she begged me to take her back. I did take her back, but it just wasn't the same between us and I ended it after about two weeks.

"But I do want a chance to catch up on things with you and, also, with some of the other discussion group members."

"Yeah, Howie, I'm definitely going. Are you bringing anyone to the party?"

"Mona said she'll take a pass on it. Is there anyone you plan to bring?"

"No, I have no current significant other to bring to the party. It'll be just me. It's great that we'll be able to get together. I'm very much looking forward to us catching up. And it should be entertaining to see Lance's antics as the Fox."

"Probably not for me, Ralph. Lance's fox antics might indeed be entertaining, but I don't think I can ever really be entertained when I know it's Lance doing the entertainment. I'm sure you understand."

"Sure, Howie, I understand completely. Well, see you there."

Tuesday, September 25, 2018

Allen Grey and Peter Regan had finished their workouts at Mike's Gym in Astoria, Queens, and were snacking together at the gym's Wellness Café. Whenever their professional schedules made it possible—which was a few times a month—they met at Mike's for workouts and then some snacks. Allen paused halfway through his salad and showed Peter his invitation to the fox party.

"Hey Pete, did you also get this in the mail?"

His friend since their college days—actually, they were just casual acquaintances in the political discussion group at Balch, and they became good friends after graduation—smiled and nodded. "Yes, I did; the Fox is back! Are you going to Lance's party?"

"Sure! Free food, free entertainment, and some fox antics from Lance. Why not go?"

"Well, when we were seniors, and, also, after we graduated, I heard some stories that Lance was not a good guy. He had a nasty, violent streak—I mean with regard to women. I'd rather not go into it."

Allen shook his head. "I never heard anything like that. Why don't we just go and have a nice time?"

Peter nodded. "Okay, I'll see you there. Maybe there will be some nice single women there too; you never know. Hey, maybe one of us will actually get lucky that evening with one of them."

His friend smiled. "Yeah, sooner or later, one—or hopefully both—of us is bound to luck out. But I mean finding the right girl to marry, not banging her on the night we first meet."

Peter laughed. "Why can't you luck out on your first evening with a girl and also end up marrying her?"

Allen was contemplative for a few seconds; then he joined in the laughter. "Yeah, I guess you can!"

Wednesday, September 26, 2018

Former private detective Norman Richland realized immediately that the voice speaking to him on the phone was being disguised, probably through the use of an app. He could not determine whether the caller was male or female. And when he checked caller ID, the phone number had been blocked.

"Mr. Richland, you were recommended to me as someone whom I can totally rely on for absolute confidentiality. I was told to give you the code word 'sunshine.' I need you to check out a house in Great Neck—I'll give you the address. I am asking you to check out all the surveillance cameras with a view of any part of the house. Then tell me which parts of the house—and which areas around the house—would not be visible in any of the surveillance. Maybe some sections on the side of the house, for example.

"If you accept this job, I'll pay you in cash, in advance. And we'll set up a way for me to pay and to receive your report while remaining completely anonymous. I'll need the results within a week. Can you do this for me?"

"Well, Mr. or Ms. Anonymous, I will not get involved in any of this if you are planning any sort of theft at that house. Otherwise, I'll accept the job. But my fees are high, as you probably know."

The caller laughed. "No worries, I'm not considering a theft of any kind. And I know about your fees. So let's finish with any formalities, and then you can do your thing. I can get you the money—in cash, as I said—today, if necessary."

That was good enough for Norman. "Okay, Anonymous, game on!"

Tuesday, October 23, 2018, Morning

At 9:45 a.m., Amy Bell was at her office desk at the Midtown Manhattan—in the Forties, just off Ninth Avenue—headquarters of the Spy4U Services detective agency, where Amy was Vice President for Sensitive Investigations. She had finished checking her messages and replying where necessary, and she was now on the internet, checking out the latest news.

When Amy attended CCNY—from which she had graduated in 2007—she was a political science major whose career goal was to become a lawyer.

Her family was not financially well-off, and in the summer of 2003, after one year of college, Amy realized that she needed part-time employment so that she could continue her education. A neighbor told Amy that she'd heard there was a part-time job opening—mornings only—at Spy4U, and Amy jumped at that possible opportunity. The next morning, without a CV, she took the subway from Queens to the Spy4U headquarters and waited outside the office of Chester Murray, Spy4U's founder and president, until he arrived. Amy made a hackneyed presentation to Chester, telling him she'd do everything necessary to succeed at any task assigned to her.

Amy had no way of knowing that, in fact, her neighbor had been mistaken; there were no job openings. But Chester somehow saw something special in this young woman. He created a part-time a.m. job and offered it to Amy, who was so excited that she accepted Chester's job offer without inquiring about the salary.

Chester mentored Amy during her early years at Spy4U. When she graduated from CCNY—due to her Spy4U employment, it took her five years—Amy accepted Chester's offer of full-time employment at Spy4U. In fall 2009, Amy solved the murders of three fellow students in an adult education evening class she was taking at CCNY. The media took notice of Amy's accomplishments, and she briefly became a minor celebrity.

Chester did not want to lose Amy to another detective agency, so he promoted Amy to her current VP title. He never regretted this decision. Amy rapidly became a superstar at Spy4U, having solved, at this point in 2018, something like twenty murders—by now Chester had lost count—in addition to supervising three Spy4U employees and working on her other non-murder cases. Her original goal of becoming a lawyer was long gone.

Some members of the NYPD, who were familiar with Amy's impressive record of solving murders, had a nickname for her; they called her "Sherlock Bell." Amy was aware of this, and she was not pleased, even though she understood that the police detectives viewed it as a compliment.

Spy4U people were encouraged to refer to each other by using first names, but Amy always referred to Chester as Mr. Murray. When asked, she said that given his position and what he had done for her, it was inappropriate for her to call him Chester—even though nearly everyone else did so.

Amy was fixated on a particular news story she had just discovered on the internet, regarding a truly disgusting word used by a public figure she hated but whom her husband, Jeremy, actually liked—how that could be possible she still did not fully understand.

She was about to phone Jeremy and confront him with this news story when there was a knock on her open office door. It was Doreen McKenzie, one of Amy's three direct subordinates.

"Amy, I need your advice on a very personal matter."

Her supervisor nodded. "Sure, shut the door and take a seat."

This was not the first time that Doreen had come to Amy for advice. In addition to being recognized as a super sleuth, Amy had a reputation as a caring person with a deep understanding of the intricacies of interpersonal relationships. She had assisted several subordinates in this area over the years, which is what gave her this reputation.

"Amy, I think Paul is seeing someone else, and he is about to give her some sort of ring. This Thursday is our second anniversary; we had our first date on October 25, 2016. I was pretty much expecting Paul to propose and give me a ring this Thursday when he will be taking me out to dinner at Big Tony's Restaurant. There had been some things he said recently that I chose to interpret as hints. Now, I don't even think I can go to dinner with him this Thursday; it would be too painful." Doreen started to cry.

Amy gave Doreen a big hug and then sat back down when Doreen stopped crying.

"Okay, tell me what happened that has made you believe Paul is cheating on you and planning to give the other woman a ring."

"Okay, I have a very dear longtime girlfriend, Nancy, who is married to Jack, a wonderful guy. I know I can trust her. They live in Riverdale, in the Bronx, as does Paul. On this past Sunday evening, she phoned me and said that afternoon, she went into Intimate Jewelers, a high-end place near her home, to look for something to buy for Jack on the occasion of his fortieth birthday.

"Nancy started talking to one of the jewelers, and then she realized that Paul was talking to another jeweler, several feet away. If he noticed her, Paul would recognize her, but she didn't think Paul realized she was there. She asked her jeweler to please be quiet for a few moments, as she wanted to pick up what Paul was saying.

"What she heard was shocking. Paul clearly still did not know she was there, because he picked up his voice a bit. He was saying that while he was not sure of her exact ring size, it had to be a relatively large size because she had relatively large, thick fingers. My friend could also see, on the counter, right next to Paul, what looked—from a distance—like the kind of diamond ring that could very well be given to a woman as an engagement ring.

"Now, Amy, of course you know that I am a relatively petite woman, with small, thin fingers. And of course, Paul knows that too. So what was likely an engagement ring—and was, in any case, a gift diamond ring—was intended, by Paul, to be given to someone else. I feel totally betrayed and humiliated."

"Doreen, has there been any kind of behavior change in Paul over the past few months, compared to previously?"

She shook her head. "No, the only change is that, as I said, Paul seemed to be hinting recently about soon proposing to me, although not in those words."

Amy was silent for a while, clearly in deep thought, with her head in her hands. Then suddenly, she cried out, "Oh my god, I know what happened! Oh my god! Doreen, I obviously cannot be 100 percent sure, but I am at least 95 percent confident that on this coming Thursday—or at least on some day in the very near future—Paul will produce a ring and propose to you! It was one small thing you said that led me to understand what happened in that jewelry store!

"So you have to go to Big Tony's on Thursday for dinner with Paul. And, by the way, Big Tony's is one of our favorite restaurants. After you two become engaged, the four of us have to arrange a dinner date at Big Tony's."

Doreen looked confused. "Amy, I want to be as confident as you are, but I can't see how you came to this conclusion. Can you explain? And what was the 'small thing' that tipped you off?"

Her supervisor nodded. "Here's what happened: Contrary to what Nancy believed, Paul recognized Nancy soon after she entered the store, and he was pretty sure that she recognized him too. This did not make him happy, as he was in the process of buying an engagement ring for you, and he wanted to surprise you with his proposal—probably this coming Thursday. He felt that he could not trust Nancy to keep this confidential, even if he explained the situation to her.

"So he pretended that he did not see Nancy, and when she became quiet, he raised his voice—to make sure that she would hear—and he started talking about the only thing he could immediately think of that might get Nancy off the trail. He pretended that the intended recipient had relatively big, thick fingers—clearly not your fingers. He hoped that when she heard this, Nancy would assume that the ring was for some relative of Paul's, to mark some special occasion, and was not intended as an engagement ring. Or, possibly, Paul was acting as the agent for a friend, who was the actual buyer of the ring.

"In the very brief time Paul had to decide what to do, he did not consider the likelihood that Nancy would assume that the ring was intended for some other woman whom Paul had been secretly dating. It should have crossed his mind, but it didn't.

"The 'small thing' that locked it up for me was when you told me Nancy said that when she became silent, Paul raised his voice. Either I'm spot-on with all this or that's one damned hell of a coincidence."

Doreen smiled and nodded. "You know, it makes sense. I'm not 95 percent sure, like you are, but I'll accept that explanation as very likely the correct one, and I'll go to dinner with Paul at Big Tony's on Thursday. And if, as I hope and pray, Paul proposes and presents me with a ring, I'll act very surprised.

"Thank you so much, Amy, for working this out for me. If not for you, I might well have done something I'd always regret."

Amy smiled. "It was my pleasure." But she thought to herself, *Oh god, I hope I'm right!*

Doreen departed, but Chester immediately arrived at Amy's office to discuss an issue regarding a current investigation. Amy realized that her phone call to Jerry—that was the nickname she generally used for her husband—would have to wait.

Tuesday, October 23, 2018, Afternoon

At one forty-five, Amy was done with lunch, had handled all her pressing obligations, and was ready to school her husband about how evil someone he liked actually was. She knew, from similar past encounters during their eight-and-a-half-year marriage, that it was probably a waste of time to discuss anything political with Jeremy, but in this case, she had to do it.

Amy's family had a long tradition of progressive liberalism, and her parents had successfully inculcated those political values in their daughter. This also resulted in a trait that her parents had not tried to instill; Amy often became an intolerant bully in political discussions with those who disagreed with her.

Amy had not forgotten that due to politics, she almost permanently ended her relationship with Jeremy on the Friday evening, in March 2007, when they had first met.

Jeremy's friend Eddie Mitchell, whom he had known since they were school children in Columbus, Ohio, had convinced Jeremy to accompany him to Marty's, an East Side singles bar. Jeremy, at age twenty-five, was five foot eleven and classically handsome. But he was quite shy with women and hadn't had too much success with them. Eddie, while not that handsome, had a likeable, outgoing personality with women.

Shortly after entering Marty's, they noticed two women sitting at a table for four with two empty seats. The women were Amy and her friend Cathy, who, at that time, were sharing an apartment in

Astoria, Queens. Eddie thought that Cathy looked very attractive, and he told Jeremy they should walk over, take the empty seats, and Jeremy should talk to the girl wearing glasses—who was Amy—as he liked the other one. Jeremy followed instructions.

After a few minutes of chitchat, Amy—who was five foot four, with brown hair, and three years younger than Jeremy—suggested that the two of them should find a secluded table for two upstairs. Jeremy happily obliged, and the conversation blossomed upstairs until Amy asked Jeremy who—not counting relatives and friends—was the twentieth-century person he most admired. After a bit of thought, Jeremy's response was Ronald Reagan.

It was all downhill from there. Before long, Amy had called Jeremy a reactionary and a self-hating Jew—among other epithets. She told him that she was also Jewish, and no self-respecting Jew could admire Reagan or even be any kind of conservative. Amy went on and on and sounded very angry. She expanded the field of play by loudly hurling insults directed toward President George W. Bush and Attorney General John Ashcroft, as well as toward anyone—such as Jeremy in particular—who approved of them.

After several minutes of this, Amy said she was going downstairs to get her coat. Jeremy took this to mean that Amy was no longer interested in him and was ending their very brief relationship and planning to go home—and, anyhow, she was a total nutcase to boot. Jeremy had originally brought his coat upstairs with him, so, having already paid for the drinks, he went down a rear staircase, left via the back door, and went home, depressed, as he had liked Amy a lot before she exploded.

But Jeremy had—understandably—totally misunderstood Amy's intentions. Amy had found Jeremy to be very good-looking and interesting, and when she got downstairs, she told that to Cathy and Eddie, who had also hit it off. Amy told Cathy that she wanted to take Jeremy back to their apartment that evening if Cathy wanted to do likewise with Eddie. The two women had an arrangement, regarding the two of them going together to a singles bar, that it would either be both of them bringing guys back to their apartment that evening, or else neither.

Cathy said fine, so Amy went back upstairs to invite Jeremy to the apartment, but she discovered that Jeremy was gone. She was very upset and had to tell Cathy and Eddie the bad news. This meant that Eddie could not go to the apartment with Cathy, which, of course, came as an unexpected blow to him.

The next morning, Saturday, Jeremy received an angry, frustrated phone call from Eddie, who told him everything that had happened after Jeremy left by the back door. Eddie pleaded with his friend to contact Amy as soon as possible and to "make things right" between them.

So at one in the afternoon, Amy answered the phone and heard Jeremy's voice. "Will you accept a sincere apology from your favorite Jewish fascist?" She laughed and invited Jeremy to come over to her apartment at around six o'clock that evening, and they would "go out somewhere."

He did go to Amy's apartment, but they never left. Instead, at Amy's initiation, they made love, twice. Jeremy didn't get back to his apartment until mid-afternoon on Sunday. At that time, he phoned Eddie and said he was pretty confident that he made things right with Amy.

This was the start of a torrid romance of several months' duration, followed by a much longer period when Amy and Jeremy were friends with benefits. Finally, in fall 2009, they both realized that they had loved each other all along, and they became engaged, with marriage occurring in January 2010.

When people asked Amy how she could end up marrying a conservative, she usually responded that sometimes, God smacks you in the ass and there's nothing you can do about it.

Jeremy was a freelance actuarial consultant who usually worked out of their two-bedroom, two-bath Greenwich Village co-op apartment. Amy viewed him as a math genius; her husband knew that wasn't even close to being true, but he did not dispute her. Eddie and Cathy eventually also married and remained at the Astoria apartment that Cathy and Amy had shared. Eddie was now a detective in the NYC Police Department, and Amy often requested his assistance in solving one of her Spy4U murder cases. Shortly after her marriage to Jeremy, Amy had successful laser eye surgery and no longer needed to wear glasses.

Jeremy picked up the phone. "Hi sweetheart, what's going on?"

"Well, Jerry, I think I may have just saved a potential marriage. This coming Thursday, I may find out for sure. I'll tell you all about it when I get home. But what I want to tell you now is what your vile, disgusting president—whom you voted for—said at a Houston rally yesterday evening. He flatly stated, 'I am a nationalist.' And everyone knows exactly what he meant by that dog whistle."

Her husband laughed—he knew that would drive Amy nuts. "Yeah, Trump means that he will not allow other countries, even our friends, to take advantage of us, economically, with regard to trade, or measures to mitigate climate change, or even payment, by every NATO member, of their share of NATO dues. Trump was not my first choice for GOP presidential candidate in 2016—that was Governor Walker—but this is just one example of how Trump is doing a very good job as president."

He specifically used the word "Trump" frequently, as he knew that his wife, "on principle," refused to ever use it, and, instead, used phrases like "your president."

"Jerry, you know full well that 'nationalist' is a dog whistle which means 'white supremacist' and 'xenophobe.' It's like in Charlottesville where he said there were fine people on both sides."

He briefly laughed again. "Sweetheart, that had to do with tearing down statues. But when you go after Trump like this, I fully understand that it is actually your dog whistle, to alert us to the fact that you have a big sexual thing for him!" Now, Jeremy burst into a round of hysterical laughter; after about five seconds of this, Amy hung up in disgust.

There you go, God, she muttered, *smacking me on the ass again!*

Amy's frustration, directed at the Almighty, was short-lived. Her office phone rang; it was Chester, calling from his office. "Amy, can you come over to my office now? There's someone here who wants to ask you and Spy4U to investigate a murder. As always, with murder cases, it will be your call as to whether you accept the case."

She immediately perked up. "A murder? Sure, Mr. Murray, I'll be right over." Amy immediately forgot about Trump and Jeremy. Her heart started racing; she was breathing rapidly. The thought of a new murder case always did this to her.

When she entered Chester's office, the boss's guest rose from his seat and shook Amy's hand. He was six feet tall, in excellent shape, appearing to be in his early forties. Amy took a third seat, close to where the other two were sitting, and the guest began his presentation.

"Amy—Chester says I should call you Amy—my name is George Canfield; of course, you can call me George. I'm a senior vice president at Arno Consulting; we have offices in a number of major cities, including our headquarters, here, in midtown Manhattan. We provide some very beneficial services for companies, and, in 2011, we asked Lance Redding to join our firm as part of our special team, dedicated to recruitment, namely convincing companies whom we are confident would greatly benefit from our assistance to become our clients.

"Lance was very successful in this role. He and I also became good friends. He always invited me to his—generally annual—fox parties, at his home in Great Neck, where he dressed up in a full-body fox outfit, including a smiling fox head, did some comedy, and had other live entertainment. There was also a catered buffet, for the guests' dining pleasure, and, also, a variety of drinks, with bar service. The most recent fox party was on Saturday, October 6, of this year, from 5:00 to 9:00 p.m.

"For each fox party, Lance selected a different special group of guests to invite, in addition to some regulars, such as myself. This time, it was former fellow members of the Balch College political discussion group during his senior year at Balch. Each of the invitees could bring along an additional guest, and two of the six discussion group members who came to the party did so.

"The party went very well—to the best of my knowledge. Lance took off his fox head a few times, revealing his big smile. The guests all left between 8:45 and 9:05 p.m. Lance hung around outside his house, in his fox outfit, to greet the guests as they arrived and, also, to say goodbye as they departed. It was obvious that he truly loved being dressed in that outfit! Of course, I already knew that from work, and several guests said he was the same way at Balch College. They said that he did not seem to want to remove the outfit unless he absolutely had to.

"I drove straight home, arriving at about nine forty, and spent the rest of the evening with my wife Arlene, who never wants to attend company events unless it is absolutely necessary. And, more importantly, we have two young children, and she does not like to unnecessarily hire a babysitter.

"The next morning, Sunday, Lance was supposed to meet two of our Arno people at eleven thirty for brunch at a Great Neck restaurant. When he did not show up and did not answer his phone nor respond to texts, they drove to his house, where they tried the front door but found it locked, and no one answered when they rang the bell.

"Then one of them remembered that Lance, like many other Arno colleagues, had provided the firm with the name of a neighbor to whom he had given a spare key to his home in case of emergency. They contacted this neighbor, who came over and used the key to open Lance's front door—this was at around two in the afternoon. They discovered Lance on the floor in the dining room, shot to death, with multiple bullet wounds, and with the apparent murder weapon lying next to him. He was still in his fox outfit, but without the fox head; one shot was through the outfit, and the others hit his head. There was blood on the floor and, of course, on the fox outfit. They contacted the police, who, so far, seem to have made very little progress in solving the murder.

"I have a contact—who is also a friend—in the Nassau County Police, in their Manhasset Precinct. He is Detective Charles Livingston. He has—sort of—confirmed their lack of progress. He told me there was no DNA or fingerprints on the gun, and that the murder likely occurred sometime around midnight. He also told me that if I hire a private detective to work on the case, he'll be happy to cooperate, as much as possible.

"I also contacted all the guests at the party—Lance had provided each of us with a guest list—and they all said they were shocked to hear that Lance was killed, and they'd be happy to cooperate in any investigation of the murder by any private detective whom I might hire. Amy, I am hoping that you will accept the case. I owe it to Lance to do what I can to help solve his murder."

Amy was a little confused. "George, why do the police say it happened around midnight? Was the medical examiner that specific? Otherwise, I would suspect that one of the party guests came back shortly after everyone left to have it out with Lance about something, and then that guest shot him."

George smiled. "Good question. As I recall, I was told that the medical examiner said death occurred between 8:00 p.m. and 1:00 a.m. But a surveillance camera showed that at around eleven o'clock, Lance, still in his full fox costume, opened the front door of his house, went outside, and pranced around for a few minutes before going back inside."

"Is there any video of someone entering and/or leaving the house after the party guests had left?"

"No one entered or exited from the front door after the party guests left, except for Lance, at eleven o'clock. There is also a back door, with video surveillance, but it was never opened at any time between the start of the party and when the body was found.

"The police discovered that one window, in the den, on the side of the house, was unlocked. It was in a place where it would not be visible with either of the two surveillance cameras. And there was substantial evidence that someone entered and exited the home via that window."

"George, is there a burglar alarm system, where an alarm bell would go off, and/or the police would be notified?"

"Yes, but I've been told that Lance did not turn it on, except when he went to bed for the night, or when he left the house for a significant period of time. I think that's the way most people act; they generally don't leave it on when they are at home during the day, or even during the evening, prior to going to bed."

"So do the police think that some guest at the party unlocked the window when no one was looking, and then he or she returned between eleven and one o'clock, entered through that window, shot and killed Lance, and then exited via the same window? In that case, wouldn't a surveillance camera catch the murderer as they arrived and departed?"

"The police say there would have been a route, along the woods behind the house, where the cameras would not catch the killer. And yes, your scenario was favored by the police, but Detective Livingston told me it seems that all the party guests have good alibis for the time between eleven and one—I certainly do, thank goodness. He said to keep that information confidential, except for telling any private detective whom I may hire. And that's where I think the police are stuck at this point."

"Is there any obvious motive for the killing?"

"Yes, Amy, there may be a clear motive. Ever since college, Lance has gone after many women, sometimes stealing other men's girlfriends. As the Fox, he was irresistible to many women—or so I've been told. Also, there are stories that he mistreated some of the women he was with, even being violent at times. He had two very brief marriages, both ending when his wife filed for divorce. So there could be a whole bunch of people—both men and women—who might have had a serious grudge against Lance."

"So does that mean the police now believe that someone who was not at the party coincidentally chose the day of the party to show up between eleven and one o'clock at night, found a side window open, entered through that window, shot and killed Lance, and then exited through that window?"

George laughed. "The way you put it, that sequence of events sounds very improbable. There may be a better possibility, namely that one of the party guests' alibis is not as good as we had thought."

Amy nodded. "Makes sense." She glanced at Chester, who also nodded. "Okay, I'll accept the case. Can you get in touch with Detective Livingston and let him know that I would like to meet with him—presumably at the Manhasset Precinct—as soon as possible?"

"Will do. And thank you so much for accepting the case. I don't expect miracles—although of course I would be thrilled if you did, in fact, accomplish a miracle. But, as I said, I owe this to Lance. And

I'll contact all the partygoers about my hiring you and your firm. I'll also tell them it's fine to use first names."

Amy exited Chester's office to let the two men work out the final details. When she got back to her office, she phoned her husband. "Jerry, Jerry! I'll be investigating a new murder case! I'll tell you everything when I get home. Pick up a large pizza with pepperoni and meatballs for dinner. And, also, a container of chocolate chip ice cream."

"Okay, sweetheart, will do. And don't forget that you also want to tell me about Doreen."

She laughed. "You know, I had actually forgotten about that! I'll tell you about Doreen first, to get it out of the way. After that, I'll go over the new murder case. And it's a really mysterious situation; I'll definitely need your help."

Jeremy had indeed assisted Amy in solving some of her previous murder cases. There were several cases where he had said something that he thought was totally insignificant, and Amy had screamed something like, "Oh my god, Jerry! You just solved the case." Then she explained everything to him so he could see how what he said gave her the solution.

"No problem, sweetheart, it should be an interesting evening for me."

Tuesday, October 23, 2018, Evening

They had finished their chocolate chip ice cream and moved to the living room. Amy related to her husband what had transpired that morning regarding Doreen and her boyfriend Paul. "So, Jerry, what do you think? Do you agree with my conclusion?"

He nodded vigorously. "Oh yeah, I'm 99 percent confident—that's even higher than your percent—that you're right. What saddens me is that Doreen—and so many other people too—are willing to jump to the conclusion that someone they love and/or respect has done a terrible thing when there are other reasonable explanations for what has occurred.

"Doreen said that Paul had done nothing whatsoever to indicate that he might be seeing someone else. In fact, she interpreted some things Paul said to her recently as hints that he was about to propose in the near future. So then, how could she immediately jump to the worst possible interpretation of what her friend saw and heard in the jewelry store?"

Amy nodded. "You're right, Jerry, but I think it's mainly because many women are very insecure. They have a low self-image, which gets them to think that they are not physically attractive enough—or don't have a good enough personality—to keep a desirable guy from looking elsewhere."

"Well, sweetheart, you would be in a better position than me to understand women's insecurities, so I accept your explanation. But, believe me, there are lots of insecure guys; I'm sure you've heard men say they could never succeed with a particular girl because she's out of their league. Heck, I originally thought that you were out of my league. But on my first visit to your apartment, you did a good job relieving me of that opinion." They both laughed.

"Jerry, that's one hell of a double entendre, where you used the phrase 'relieving me'! Do you realize it?" Now, they again both burst into laughter.

When they calmed down, Amy continued. "That's a great lead-in for my new murder case. The murder victim was a guy who was the exact opposite of being insecure regarding women. Lance Redding was self-confident with women, to the extreme. He was a chick-magnet who also mistreated some of the women who were attracted to him, and that may well have been the reason why he was murdered."

She related to her husband the presentation made that afternoon by George Canfield. "So, Jerry, do you have any first impressions?"

He nodded. "I would say that it's very highly likely that one of the party guests came back a few hours later and shot Lance. That way, the killer knew to unlock the side window during the party when no one was watching. If the killer was someone not at the party, who had a grudge against Lance, that means he or she was extraordinarily lucky that, for some reason, that window was unlocked. And, also, it just happened to be two or three hours after the party—where there could be some logical suspects—broke up. It's all theoretically possible, but extremely unlikely."

Now Amy nodded. "So you're saying that one of the party guests probably has a phony alibi for the period between eleven and one o'clock."

"That's right. Maybe the killer got one or more people to lie and say he—or she—was with them at the time of the murder. It's even possible that there were two co-conspirators at the party, who jointly planned the murder and became each other's phony alibis. By the way, do you think you'll be able to polygraph any of the party guests?"

Amy smiled. "Regarding phony alibis, I'll have to see how airtight the party guests' alibis are. And I doubt I'll have enough leverage to get any of them to agree to take lie detector tests; but we'll see. By the way, couldn't the killer be someone not at the party who got one of the party guests to open the side window for him?"

Jeremy smiled. "Yes, that's also theoretically possible, but I'll still go with the killer being a party guest. So whom do you plan to speak to first?"

"I guess that would be Detective Charles Livingston of the Nassau County Police. He has been George's contact regarding Lance's murder. After that, I want to speak to all the party guests. Even if they have seemingly perfect alibis, I want to get their input. Then there are Lance's two former wives."

"Sweetheart, do you know of any other possible motive to murder Lance?"

"No, not at this point. But after I talk to the detective and to the party guests, I may come up with some other possible motive—or motives."

"You're a woman. Does it make sense to you that a guy who loved prancing around in a full-body fox costume was, for the past decade, a chick magnet?"

"Jerry, I can say with confidence that it makes no sense to me whatsoever!" They both burst into laughter.

Thursday, October 25, 2018

At three fifteen in the afternoon, Nassau County Police Detective Charles Livingston ushered Amy Bell into his office at the Manhasset Police Precinct. He took the seat at his desk, and Amy sat on the other side, facing him. Charles appeared to be in his fifties, was of average height, and was somewhat overweight. He had a big, welcoming smile on his face. The detective initiated the conversation.

"My friend George Canfield said he retained you and your firm to investigate the murder of Lance Redding. As I told him, I'll be very happy to update you, as much as I am permitted, regarding the state of our investigation, which can be fairly described as being somewhat stalled at this point.

"By the way, please call me Charles, and I have a question: should I call you Amy or Sherlock?" He immediately burst into laughter.

Amy smiled diplomatically. "I prefer Amy. I guess you know some NYC police detectives."

Charles smiled. "Yes, I do. And a few of them have told me all about you. So I'll give you the rundown on the Lance Redding case. At 2:10 p.m. on Sunday, October 7 of this year, we received a 911 call saying that Lance had been found shot dead in his home in Great Neck. We arrived at 2:25 and found a body identified as Lance—five foot ten and 165 pounds—lying dead on the floor of his dining room. He was still wearing the fox outfit, which, we understand, he was wearing at a party at his home that he threw the previous evening. Except he was not wearing the fox head, which was found in his bedroom.

He had been shot three times—twice in the head and once in the back. The medical examiner said death had been instantaneous.

"What was later determined to be the murder weapon, a 9 mm Springfield Echelon handgun, was found lying near the body. There were no fingerprints or DNA on the gun. It turned out that the gun had been stolen, two years ago, from its legal owner, who lived in Mobile, Alabama. This owner had, at the time of the theft, reported it to the local police.

"In the den, there was a window, which we discovered was unlocked, facing toward the side of the house. There were indications that the window had been used by someone to enter and/or leave the house. All the other windows in the house were locked, as was the rear door. We learned that the front door had also been locked until a neighbor with a key opened it a few minutes prior to our arrival.

"The burglar alarm had not been turned on. There were two surveillance cameras outside the house, with views of the front and back door areas. We checked out the videos, and they showed that after the guests left the party, no one entered or exited either door until Lance's friends arrived at 2:00 p.m. on October 7.

"The only exception was Lance himself, dressed in his full-body fox costume with smiling fox head—which he had basically worn through nearly the entire duration of his party—who exited via the front door at 11:05 p.m., walked and danced around the immediate front area, and then reentered the house via the same door at 11:10 p.m. Neighbors told us that Lance had a reputation for that kind of behavior at various hours during the day. For some weird reason, he loved wearing and parading around in that suit." They both laughed, and then he continued.

"Lance had invited all fifteen members—besides Lance himself—of the Balch College political discussion group during his senior year. Six of them accepted his invitation.

"We interviewed those six guests, as well as the two people invited by two of the discussion group members—one by each member—to join them at the party. Two women, Doris Mays and her guest, Marilyn Waller, said that when the party ended, they immediately drove home in Doris's car. The two women said they hung out together at Marilyn's home until one in the morning, and then Doris drove back to her home.

"The other five discussion group members—plus one lady who was Lance's colleague at Arno Consultants—agreed to meet at McCloud's Tavern, in Kew Gardens, Queens, at around ten fifteen p.m. for some after-party food and/or drinks and for some additional political and other conversation. This would allow any of them—at least those who lived reasonably close to anywhere on the route between Great Neck and the tavern—to stop at their respective homes to change clothes or check in with their spouses or whatever before showing up at the tavern. It also allowed one group member to drive home the person he brought with him to the party and then head for the tavern. Of course, some guests had no reason to go anywhere else, and they showed up at the tavern a bit earlier than ten fifteen.

"They all confirmed that all six of them were there, together, at the tavern, between 10:25 p.m. and 12:55 a.m. No one of the six was out of their sight for any prolonged period of time.

"In addition to George, two gentlemen partygoers were colleagues of Lance at Arno Consulting, as was the lady who joined the discussion group members at the tavern. Those two men both said they drove straight home to their spouses, who would, if necessary, confirm that the two of them were home, together, from around ten p.m. on. And that rounds out the guest list."

Now Charles smiled. "There is one possibly significant piece of evidence that I have not yet mentioned. There were no fingerprints or DNA on the unlocked den window, but there were a small number of fibers that appeared to have rubbed off from a glove. We presume that the killer wore gloves when he or she opened the window, to avoid leaving prints. We haven't been able to determine whether the fibers came from men's gloves or women's gloves. Please keep this completely confidential."

Amy nodded. "Of course."

"Do you have any questions?"

"Charles, can you give me the contact information for all the party guests, as well as for Lance's two former wives? George told me that Lance actually handed out this contact information—except regarding his wives—to the party guests, but your information would probably be more thorough and reliable."

He nodded. "I sure will, Amy."

"Do you have any photos of Lance, wearing the fox outfit and, also, wearing regular street clothes?"

"Sure, I'll get you a few photos."

"Do you know who inherits Lance's money and property?"

"As I understand it, everything goes to charity. Lance had no living close relatives—except for two former wives, of course." They both laughed.

"Charles, how easy is it to enter through that side window? And wouldn't there be a good chance some neighbor might see what's going on?"

"Good questions. I'd say the average person would want to bring a small stool to stand on when entering. That's probably what the killer did; then they left with the stool after exiting. At night, with quite a distance between homes, I'd say it was unlikely that a neighbor would notice, although there would always be that possibility."

"Didn't the party have lots of food and drinks? I'm wondering how those six guests could all go to the tavern that same evening for more food and drinks."

"As I understand it, the food and drink aspect ended at 7:30 p.m. That's when the caterer, who handled all that stuff, cleaned up, packed up, and left. After that was the entertainment—including Lance, doing antics in his fox costume—until eight forty-five. There were two musicians, who packed up and left before nine o'clock. So I guess that by ten fifteen, those six guests were ready for more alcoholic beverages and possibly for a few small snacks to go with the drinks. Of course, they could have done most of their eating and/or drinking at around eleven, or even later than that.

"Also, it's certainly possible that two or three of them went to the tavern solely because they enjoyed everyone's company and political conversations; they each may have ordered one perfunctory drink, so as not to look bad."

She nodded. "Yeah, Charles, I guess that makes some sense. It just bothers me that they all have this perfect alibi. But I guess that's just how it is.

"One final question for now, on another topic. Has any woman ever brought charges against Lance, claiming he was physically violent toward her?"

"Not as far as I am aware. I'll check that out further, and if there were any such charges, I'll let you know.

"And, Amy, if you come up with any additional questions, please don't hesitate to contact me."

They shook hands, and Amy departed for home. After dinner, she discussed with her husband what Detective Livingston had told her.

"So, Jerry, that's quite an alibi that those six guests have; they were all together at McCloud's Tavern between 10:25 p.m. and 12:55 a.m."

He nodded. "Yeah, that looks pretty ironclad. Then you have the two lady guests who came together to the party and say they drove home together right after the party. Unless they're in it together, they also seem to be in the clear as suspects. You may have to look at some other possible suspects, including his two former wives."

"Jerry, you're sure as hell right about that. And of course, there could be some woman whom he badly abused at some point during the past decade—maybe recently—who finally decided to kill him and just happened to do it on the same evening as the party."

"But, sweetheart, how did that woman know the side window would be open?"

Amy was contemplative for a few seconds, then she responded. "Maybe she checked out the house—or had someone else check out the house—several days previously, discovered that one side window was unlocked, and hoped that Lance would not realize it until she had a chance to enter via that window and murder him."

"Sweetheart, one of those badly abused women might have retained a hired killer to shoot Lance. I think that might actually make more sense than saying the woman actually climbed in through the window and shot him."

She nodded. "Could be, you do have a point."

At 7:20 p.m., Amy's phone rang. It was Doreen. Amy put on the speaker, so Jeremy could hear. "Amy, Amy! You were right! I'm calling you from the ladies' room at Big Tony's. Paul proposed to me and gave me a ring! I think it's the same ring that Nancy saw when Paul pretended it was for a woman with thick fingers. Amy, you saved me from making a terrible mistake. I am forever in your debt."

"Hey, Doreen, what's a supervisor for? I'm here to help you!" They both laughed heartily. "Just make sure that Jerry and I are invited to your wedding."

"Amy, that's for sure! I've got to get back to Paul, so I'll get off. Oh god, I love you—not like I love Paul, but I love you!" They both laughed, and then they got off the phone.

"Jerry, you heard that, right?"

"You bet! I'm not at all surprised, and I'm sure that you aren't surprised either. But it's still a big relief that Paul actually did propose at the dinner, as Doreen had suspected would happen until the jewelry store incident occurred. So I guess we're going to their wedding."

She nodded. "Well, I'm sure we'd have been invited even if the jewelry store incident had never occurred. Now, I wouldn't be surprised if she asks me to be a bridesmaid."

"Sweetheart, would that be a good thing, or would it really be a big, unpleasant hassle that you would be too embarrassed to decline?"

She laughed. "If she asks me to be a bridesmaid, I'll take it as an honor that I would be delighted to receive. In any case, do you have the same feeling that I have, namely that there's something very weird about this entire Lance Redding murder case?"

Her husband smiled and nodded. "I sure do. It somehow just doesn't make sense to me. But Lance was, indeed, murdered, so I guess there will be a logical explanation. I hope that you can find it. So are you planning to start by interviewing the six guests who were at the tavern?"

"Yes, I think they should be the first people I speak to. I'll go through the list the detective gave me and arrange some interviews."

Saturday, October 27, 2018

At one fifteen in the afternoon, Amy rang the doorbell at the Flushing, Queens, ranch home of Jean and Bill Santori. When she spoke to Bill on the phone, that was the date and time he suggested, and Amy was happy to oblige. Jeremy was not going to be home until around three o'clock, as he was playing his usual Saturday tennis doubles games with his regular doubles partner—and his regular opponent, when he played singles—Jason Linker.

They sat in the dining room, where Amy accepted a Coke Zero and some chocolate chip cookies. Amy knew that the Santoris were, like most of the party guests, in their early thirties. She felt that they were acting unusually "lovey-dovey" with each other, so she came right out and asked, "Have you guys been married for just a brief period of time?"

Bill was impressed. "Wow, how did you guess that? Or did you do some research and find our wedding date on the Internet?"

Amy laughed. "Actually, I did not do any research. I just watched the way you two acted toward each other. How long have you been married?"

Jean smiled. "Four months. I am so lucky that I found Bill. My whole adult life, I had dreamed of being married to someone like Bill." She pointed at her husband. "And now, here he is!"

Bill laughed. "I feel the same way; it's a first marriage for both of us. Jean is what I'd always prayed for but never expected would ever happen for me."

Amy nodded. "Well, congratulations. So, Bill, please tell me about the party and what you may know about Lance."

"Okay, I knew Lance starting when we were both juniors at Balch College in Valley Stream. I met him that September when we both joined the political discussion group. There was nothing unusual about him at that time. He was relatively quiet and did not speak up as much as some others in the group. His politics were relatively middle-of-the-road.

"We had all signed a pledge to be respectful of the political views of all members and to never demean anyone, regardless of how strongly we opposed them, politically. And we all stuck by that pledge, so the group was a very enjoyable experience. But, as I said, Lance was hardly noticed by most of us.

"All that changed in the spring semester of our junior year. Lance became the mascot for our college baseball and basketball teams. He wore a full-body smiling fox costume, and he appeared at the games those teams played, leading cheers. He also sometimes wore that outfit around the campus, sometimes in class and at our discussion group.

"And his personality changed. He became self-confident and gregarious, particularly with female students, many of whom suddenly seemed to find him irresistible. As I understand it, he dated a whole lot of Balch College female students, mainly during his senior year.

"After Lance graduated from Balch, no student stepped forward to wear a fox costume, but Lance sometimes returned to Balch to reprise his role as the Fox. I understand that Lance sometimes wore a fox costume while at work, and he also sometimes paraded around his Great Neck neighborhood in that outfit. I was told that he actually had several fox costumes, with various sleeve lengths, that he kept in a closet under lock and key when not in use.

"In September, I received Lance's invitation to a fox party on October 6. The invitation said he had invited all the members of the Balch College political discussion group during our senior year. This was the first fox party where he invited members of our discussion group, so I was anxious not only to see Lance display his fox antics again, but also to reconnect with some members of our discussion group, whom I hadn't had any contact with for a decade.

"Jean, understandably, told me that she would rather visit her sister than go to this party. In a sense, I was lucky that she felt that way, because I enjoy drinking alcoholic beverages a lot more than Jean does, so she would not have wanted to go to the tavern after the party was over.

"And the tavern turned out to be the best part of the evening for me. Sure, the food and drinks at the party were great, and Lance was very funny, but my favorite aspect was renewing my political discussions with the group members, and we did that, in spades, at the tavern, much more than earlier, at the party.

"I left the tavern at ten minutes past one in the morning, promising myself never to again lose contact with the other five tavern-goers. As Jean was staying overnight at her sister's, I did not have to worry about getting home at one thirty. And that's my story."

Amy nodded. "Thank you so much, Bill, for your detailed presentation. I have a question. Do you know of—or did you hear gossip about—Lance being abusive to some of the women he dated?"

Bill nodded. "Interesting that you would ask me that. I have no definitive knowledge, but, starting in our senior year, I heard a bunch of stories about women being treated very badly by Lance, including physical violence in some cases. I heard about one girl who actually had her nose broken by Lance. But please understand, I heard all this stuff third-hand. I can't confirm the accuracy of anything.

"I do know that both of Lance's ex-wives divorced him, claiming physical and mental abuse, but I also know that there are some women who fabricate these kinds of claims when in a divorce situation. I also heard that there was a woman who left Lance after several months living with him and then committed suicide shortly after she moved out. I do not have any other information, such as her name, so this story could easily be false, and, also, even if she did kill herself, Lance may not have been in any way responsible for the suicide.

"I know people can say that where there's smoke there's fire, but I would hate to have gullible people believe such stories about me, maybe spread by people jealous of my accomplishments—I'm a very successful attorney. But, since you asked, I told you what I've heard over the years."

Jean spoke up. "To say that Bill is very successful would be a gross understatement! And I also want to point out that Bill has told me Lance was also very successful—as a popular guy with the gals and also at his job—so people might have spread false stories about Lance because they were very jealous of him."

Amy smiled and nodded. "Jean, that's a very good point. Bill, can you think of any motive for someone killing Lance, other than the possibility that a woman had been badly abused by him, and so, she decided to kill him?"

Bill considered Amy's question for a few seconds, and then he responded. "Well, as we understand it, Lance was very successful at his job with Arno Consultants, which was primarily soliciting new client companies. Maybe someone at Arno wanted Lance's job, and as there were no openings in that department, they murdered Lance to create a job opening.

"Or, maybe, Lance knew something very bad about one of his colleagues, and that individual felt that they had to kill Lance to keep it a secret.

"Or, maybe, some guy had developed a giant crush on a girl Lance was seeing. And he figured he would never have a chance with her if he had to compete with Lance."

Amy laughed. "Wow, Bill, there could be a promising employment opportunity for you at Spy4U, helping us to solve murders and other mysteries. If you ever get tired of the legal profession, be sure to contact me."

Now Bill laughed. "I will definitely call you on that offer if I ever want to change professions."

A few minutes later, Amy shook hands with Mr. and Mrs. Santori, proceeded to her car, and drove home. Jeremy was already back home when she arrived, and she related to him what Bill had told her.

"So, Jerry, what do you think? Was Lance habitually physically violent regarding many of the women he was with?"

He nodded. "Based on what you've told me, although there's no firsthand information, I'd say it's at least 95 percent likely that most of the violence stories are true. As a juror, I'd need some firsthand testimony and probably also some physical evidence to convict. But this is not a trial; it's a murder investigation."

"Jerry, we were asking each other why those six guests would want to have more food and drinks at the tavern when they had loaded up on that stuff at the party. But, based on what Bill said, I now realize that we were looking at it the wrong way. Most—if not all—of the six guests undoubtedly went to the tavern primarily to continue their friendly political discussions, which they had enjoyed so much at Balch College and which they had greatly missed in the ensuing decade. It makes perfect sense."

"Sweetheart, to use your favorite line, you're sure as hell right about that. I'm kinda surprised that neither of us thought of that before you met with Bill. It seems so obvious now, but that's Monday morning quarterbacking."

"So, Jerry, do you agree with me that the likely scenario is that a woman previously abused by Lance came back late that evening and murdered him?"

"Yes, but with reservations. Again, how did she know the window would be unlocked?"

Amy nodded. "Well, we have discussed some possibilities. Maybe she had a co-conspirator who was a guest at the party and unlocked the den window for her. Maybe she checked out the house a few days before, discovered that the den window was unlocked—probably unintentionally—and hoped that Lance would not notice this before she came back to kill him.

"Or maybe she came to the house wearing some sort of disguise, so that when she showed up on the surveillance video, her true identity could not be determined. She would have rung the front doorbell if she found that the door was locked, but first she checked the side windows and found one of them unlocked. She could have approached the house by the back route where she would not have been seen by the cameras. Of course, if she had to go to the front door, she would have shown up, but in disguise, as I said."

Her husband smiled and nodded. "Yes, any of those scenarios could be possible. One of them is likely what happened.

"Also, it's adorable that they were lovey-dovey right in front of you. And they both say how lucky they are. I love it!"

Amy nodded. "Well, they are both in their thirties and never previously had much luck with the other sex. They probably were—somewhat unrealistically—resigned to being alone for the rest of their lives. Therefore, they both view finding their spouse as a sort of miracle. I'm so very happy for them!"

At four forty-five, the phone rang. It was Cathy. Amy put on the speakerphone.

"Hi, Amy, you've always been good at geography, right?"

"Yes, why?" Amy was intrigued.

"Well, I know it's a little late to ask, but I hope you guys are free tomorrow afternoon. There's a sports bar, Wally's World-Class Sports Bar, located a few blocks from our house."

"Yeah," interrupted Amy, "I remember that place from when we lived together in your apartment."

"Well, tomorrow afternoon, they're running what they describe as a 'world class, where in the world' geography trivia contest. There are prizes for the teams that finish in the top three. They'll also have a special lunch buffet at one thirty, followed by the trivia contest at two forty-five. The buffet costs thirty dollars; drinks are, of course, extra. And the trivia—with prizes—is free to play, if you pay for the buffet. Can you and Jeremy join us? You can come up to our apartment at, say, twelve thirty and have some fun with Aurora. Then we can walk over to the tavern at one fifteen. My mom will be there to sit with Aurora while we're gone." Aurora, their daughter, was nearly five years old.

Amy had a question. "If it's a sports bar, wouldn't they want to run a sports trivia contest, as opposed to geography?"

Cathy laughed. "Yeah, they run sports trivia once or twice a month, but we're not interested, and I assume the same holds for you. Eddie and I know some geography too, so this trivia tomorrow sounds like fun."

Amy glanced at her husband, who nodded. "Cathy, you're sure as hell right about my lack of interest in sports trivia. But yeah, geography is right up our alley. Okay, we'll see you tomorrow at your apartment at around twelve thirty, and I'll try to control myself." They both laughed. Amy was referring to a recent Name That Tune contest, where she had protested that the host's answer to one of the questions was not correct.

Cathy, who also had her speakerphone on, looked at her husband. "Eddie, did you hear Amy saying she'll try to control herself?"

He laughed. "As we both know, Amy may try, but if she thinks there's an issue with one of the answers, she will find it impossible to control herself. And, while she thinks she's embarrassing us with those antics, we don't get upset at all. We find her very entertaining!"

Now Cathy laughed. "You bet, honey!"

Back at Amy and Jeremy's apartment, she received another phone call and, seeing the caller ID, excused herself and took the call in their bedroom. When she emerged, she announced to Jerry, "Guess what! I have an interview with another tavern-goer tomorrow morning. He's Ralph Kane, responding to a phone message I left for him. He said he was visiting a friend in Greenwich Village tomorrow at eleven forty-five, so could I meet him for breakfast at ten thirty at Nico's Village Diner? I said yes, but please be on time, as I also have another appointment."

"Sweetheart, that's a lucky break for you; Nico's is only a few blocks from here. And it fits perfectly with our plans to get to Cathy's apartment at twelve thirty. I'll give you a geography trivia question—I looked up the answer on the Internet while you were speaking to Cathy. Not counting Honolulu, what is the southernmost US state capital?"

Amy was silent for about thirty seconds, clearly in deep thought. "I'm not 100 percent sure, but I'd say I'm 90 percent confident that it's Austin, Texas."

He smiled. "Well, you're right. Let's hope they ask that question tomorrow."

Sunday, October 28, 2018, Morning

At ten twenty-five, Amy entered Nico's Village Diner and found Ralph Kane sitting on a sofa in the lobby. The hostess escorted them to a table, and they ordered their food and drinks.

Ralph was five foot nine and very thin. Amy felt he almost looked gaunt. After they finished ordering, Amy asked, "Ralph, are you okay?"

"Actually, I've been somewhat under the weather lately. And given that I've always been a bit thin, I know that I must look pretty bad. But my doctor told me that I'm in the recovery stage and that I'm definitely not contagious. So I wasn't gonna miss the fox party and, also, the meeting at the tavern."

"Which was the highlight for you, the party or the tavern?"

"The tavern, for sure! I used to love our discussions, back in school, at the Balch College political discussion group. No epithets, no anger, just fun—and informative—conversations. For the past ten years, after graduation, I've had nothing like that. The discussion group members who were at the party had a bit of political talk at Lance's house, but at the tavern, the six of us let it all hang out for well over two hours! I just loved it.

"I also got to reconnect with my college friend Howie Argus. We met as juniors at Balch College, and we were both in the political discussion group. Howie graduated one semester early. We used to speak regularly on the phone, generally three or four times a year, mainly about politics, and we occasionally got together, maybe once a year.

That was as close as I ever got, after graduation, to the fantastic political exchanges we had in the discussion group. But, in recent years, our contact with each other had tailed off, eventually to none. So it was great to be with Howie at the party and at the tavern. Howie and I agreed that we have to resume our conversations—at the very least."

"Have you heard any stories about Lance being physically violent with women, either before or after graduation from college?"

"Yes, Howie brought up that exact topic when I called him in September—for the first time in several years, sadly—after I received the invitation to the fox party. He told me that he was reluctant to attend the party and that he was only going because I was going.

"He said the reason for this reluctance is what Lance had done to his former girlfriend, Joan. He said that he and Joan had become exclusive for a month, just before he graduated one semester early, in January of our senior year. He said Lance knew all about him and Joan, and Lance succeeded in stealing her from him. Then he told me what happened after that, according to Joan.

"Joan told Howie she realized, too late, that Lance was only interested to see if he could get her—a conservative, religious woman—to sleep with him. He eventually succeeded in his goal. On their next date after he had sex with Joan, they were at his apartment, and he pushed her against a wall, told Joan they were through, and then dragged her out the door. Howie said he accepted Joan's plea to take her back, but it didn't work out."

"Oh my god, Ralph, oh my god! That is unbelievably evil."

"Yeah, Amy, that's basically what I said when Howie told me what happened."

"Prior to this past September, had you heard any other stories about Lance mistreating women?"

"None that I can recall—and I'm pretty sure that if I'd heard such a story, I would, indeed, recall it."

"Are you currently married?"

He smiled. "No, not now and not ever. I guess I've never met the right woman, though I've certainly tried. But—would you believe it?—a partygoer asked for my phone number! It was Marilyn, the guest of Doris, who was in our discussion group. Marilyn didn't seem to mind how thin I currently am. She came up to me, started a conversation, and, within five minutes, asked for my number.

"I told her to give me a month to put back on some weight and to then call me. She laughed and said fine."

"Wow! Ralph, who originally suggested the get-together at the tavern, to be held after the party?"

He smiled proudly. "Actually, I was the one who suggested the tavern. Several days before the party, I discussed my idea with Howie, and he thought it was a good idea. So I then contacted the other four guests who were in the political discussion group, and the response from three of the four was very positive. We ended up at the tavern with five political discussion group members and one other partygoer, who worked as a member of Lance's team at Arno Consultants. And she was just as pleasant and knowledgeable as the others."

Amy nodded. "Yeah, it was a very smart idea. Do you have a background in party-planning?" They both laughed.

"No. I was a business major in college, and right after graduation, I started working for an accounting firm in Chicago. Then two years later, I came back to Queens and set up shop as an independent accountant. No party-planning in my background."

Their meals arrived, and after they were finished, Amy paid for the both of them. She thanked Ralph for coming, they shook hands, and then they left the diner. Amy arrived home at eleven thirty, fifteen minutes before they planned to leave for Cathy's apartment.

"So, sweetheart, how did it go with Ralph?"

"Well, Ralph told me a story you won't believe." She related what Howie had told Ralph about what Lance did to Joan.

Jeremy was nonplussed. "So first Lance stole Howie's girlfriend, then he did what was necessary to get her to have sex with him, then, on their next date, he assaulted her, broke up with her, and physically threw her out of his apartment. That's unbelievable! And this guy was a chick magnet? Truly bizarre; I think he must have been mentally ill."

"Jerry, you're sure as hell right about that! Anyhow, as with Bill, Ralph said the best part of the evening was the tavern event, with over two hours of the kind of political discussions that their group had enjoyed at college."

Her husband smiled and nodded. "Yeah, as I said, once Bill brought it to our attention, it was totally obvious that's why most of them went to the tavern. And, as I also said, I'm embarrassed that we never thought of that until Bill told us."

"Jerry, on another topic, there was something I said yesterday that I realized, a bit later on, might be important in solving the case, but now—God help me—I can't remember what it was that I said. I'm very upset. For some reason, it has totally escaped my memory. I should have written it down at the time it struck me as important."

"Don't worry, sweetheart, you'll remember; just give it a little time."

"Jerry, I sure hope you're right."

Sunday, October 28, 2018, Afternoon

At one fifteen, Amy and Jeremy had put in the requisite time chatting with Cathy's mother and playing with Aurora. They joined their hosts, Cathy and Eddie, in saying their goodbyes and heading out the door of the apartment, into the hall, down three floors on the elevator, and out into the street to begin their short walk to Wally's for the buffet lunch and the geography trivia.

As they were walking, Cathy asked Amy if she was working on any interesting cases. Amy gave her a brief summary of the Lance Redding murder case; she changed the names, calling the victim John.

When Amy had finished, Cathy burst out laughing. "Are you telling me that John was previously nothing special to women, but as soon as he put on the fox costume, he became irresistible to them?"

"Yes, apparently that's exactly what happened. And, according to what I'm being told, it turned him into a horrible person—at least with regard to his relationships with many women he was with."

"And, Amy, you're saying that the guests at his party have perfect alibis for the time of the murder?"

"Well, so far, just the ones who were at the tavern. There were other people at John's party. But the party ended at nine o'clock, and the murder occurred after eleven, so it's not so clear that the partygoers are the obvious main suspects."

At this point, they arrived at Wally's after a ten-minute walk. They were escorted to a table for four—table number eleven—in a large room and observed that the room was nearly fully occupied by guests. Cathy smiled. "I made my reservation right after you guys agreed to join us. This morning, I spoke to a woman who lives in my building, and she told me that she had phoned Wally's a few minutes earlier, and they said there was no remaining availability, so she could not attend the event."

Amy was very satisfied with the food choices available on the lunch buffet—and with one item, in particular. She mainly loaded up on the pepperoni pizza and topped it off with chocolate cake for dessert. Jeremy concentrated on the roast beef, which was sliced to order. He also took some fries and then a bowl of chocolate ice cream. Cathy and Eddie went mainly for the salads, but then they capitulated and took two large portions of cinnamon apple pie back to the table. All four ordered various wines, and Amy also consumed a Coke Zero.

While enjoying the buffet, Cathy had another question for Amy. "Do any of your current suspects have a sufficient motive to have murdered John at this particular point in time?"

Amy shook her head. "Frankly, no. The guy was a louse, but why kill him now? Obviously, for the party guests who had not seen him in quite a while, that evening—when they would be in his area—was as good a time as any. But then, why wait till after eleven to kill him?"

Eddie joined the conversation. "So, Amy, does that mean you think the killer may have had a different motive, which developed recently, and the fact that the party was on the same day as the murder is just a coincidence?"

She nodded. "Yes, that may well be the case, particularly as many of the partygoers have such great alibis for the time of the murder."

At exactly two forty-five, a snappily dressed tall, somewhat chubby man, appearing to be in his forties, climbed onto a small stage and spoke into a hand-held microphone. "Hello, everyone, my name is Barry Randolph, and I'm the general manager here at Wally's. I see some new faces—for me at least—in the room, as well as many old friends.

"I hope you all enjoyed our wonderful buffet." Loud applause. "Now here are the guidelines for the geography trivia contest. First of all, no phones or communication devices of any kind. Don't use the excuse that you were calling your mother—or that she called you—to say happy birthday. Also, don't say anything loud enough for people at any other table to hear you. I will repeat each question three times, with no further repetition. The question will also appear on the TV screens located around the room. When I go on to the next question, I will not go back to any previous question.

"There will be twenty questions, each worth one point. Then you will hand in your answer sheets to me. I will then go over the answers, after which I will grade the papers. Spelling does not count, as long as it is obvious to me—in my sole judgment—that you were intending the correct answer. And on all other issues, the decision of the judge—that's me—is final. I admit that occasionally, someone at one of our trivia contests shows me appropriate evidence, and I determine that I've made an error. If so, I will correct it.

"Every team should select a team captain, who bears final responsibility for selecting the team's answer for each question, and who will speak for the team if there are any challenges to the answers that I provide.

"There will be prizes for the three highest-scoring teams. They are twenty, forty, and eighty-dollar gift certificates for Wally's, for the third, second, and first-place teams. In case of any ties, I have tiebreaker questions. Is everyone ready? Then here goes!"

The first question was to name the capital of Australia. Amy—who, to the surprise of no one, had just unilaterally declared herself to be team captain—immediately wrote down "Canberra" and showed it around. Everyone nodded.

Question Four was to name the capital of West Virginia. Eddie immediately wrote "Wheeling?" while Cathy and Jeremy had blanks on their faces. Amy smiled as she shook her head. "No, it's Charleston," she whispered. "Okay," Eddie whispered back, "it was just my best guess."

Question Six was to name the largest country entirely in Europe. Amy had no idea, but Jeremy wrote down "Ukraine" and displayed a big smile and a thumbs-up.

None of them knew the capital of Surinam, which was the next question, so Amy wrote down "Sudendam" as a wild guess. Eddie laughed and observed, "At least it sounds cute."

Question Ten was to name the tallest uninterrupted waterfall in the world. Cathy whispered, "It's Angel Falls in Venezuela; I know that for sure." The others breathed sighs of relief.

Question Thirteen was rather lengthy: "The 2020 Summer Olympics will be in Tokyo, where their native language is not English. But let's assume it is English. And assume the countries in that 2020 Olympics will be the same as in 2016. Then in the parade of nations—which is in alphabetical order—which country whose name begins with the letter M will be first when the line reaches that letter?"

Jeremy was confused. "Why go through all that? Why not just ask which country beginning with M comes first in alphabetical order?"

Amy smiled. "Because it's a trick question. Macedonia was the first M in line in 2016, but since then, they have decided to change their name to North Macedonia, which will officially take effect in 2019.

So the correct answer to the question, regarding the 2020 Summer Olympics, is Madagascar, not Macedonia."

"Good god, Amy," sighed Eddie, "how could you possibly know that kind of stuff?" Everyone laughed, as Amy smiled. "To be honest, I have no idea how I know that."

Question Sixteen was to name the most populous city in Connecticut. Amy immediately wrote down "Hartford," but Eddie corrected her. "I know for sure that it's Bridgeport. I was at a police convention recently, in Bridgeport, and they told us that fact." Amy nodded and changed her answer.

Question Eighteen was to give the final two UN member countries, when written in alphabetical order. No credit for only one of them. Jeremy immediately wrote "Zambia and Zimbabwe," and everyone agreed.

The final question was to give the total number of countries that border Germany. Amy closed her eyes for several seconds, in deep thought, and then solemnly pronounced, "It's nine." No one expressed disagreement.

They handed in their answer sheet and Amy announced, "Looks like we got eighteen right and two wrong, unless one of our wild guesses on those two questions turned out, miraculously, to be correct." The others at the table nodded in agreement.

Barry started going over the answers, and all went fine until he got to Question Thirteen and said the answer was Macedonia. Amy glanced at her teammates and then rose to protest. "I'm sorry, Barry, but you are mistaken. Macedonia's name in 2020 will be North Macedonia, not Macedonia. This has already been formally agreed to, mediated by the United Nations, as the solution to a lengthy dispute they had been having with Greece. So the correct answer to your question is

Madagascar, not Macedonia. I will be happy to show you the documentation on my iPhone."

Barry took out his own phone and spent some time checking out what Amy had said. During this time, there were snickers from many tables, where people shouted out things like "Sit down, lady," and "Get real." There was some applause, from some tables, which—Amy deduced—had written "Madagascar" as their answer. After about a minute, Barry spoke.

"The name of the country is currently still officially Macedonia. So that is the answer, and not Madagascar. Also, a preface word, such as 'North,' does not change the fact that it will still be Macedonia."

Now Amy was in a rage, and she raised her voice to a shout. "That's absurd! You specifically said the time frame was the Summer 2020 Olympics, not the present. And based on what you just said, for Question Eighteen, the final two UN countries would be Zimbabwe and Zealand, as you would throw out the preface word 'New.' Are you serious?"

Now people yelled out things like, "No, lady, are *you* serious?" and, "Get her out of here!" Barry spoke again. "Miss, please sit down now. My decision is final. The only correct answer is Macedonia."

Amy took her seat, as most of the tables broke into thunderous applause. Jeremy had his head down and Eddie and Cathy were covering their faces with their hands—actually, they were covering up their laughter, and of course, they didn't want Amy to know that.

Now, Barry finished providing the answers to the remaining questions, and then he proceeded to grade the papers, which took about fifteen minutes. When he was done, he announced the results.

"We had eighty-nine trivia players, each belonging to one of twenty-four teams, seated at twenty-four tables. There were nineteen answer sheets handed in; five tables left early without handing in their answers. The highest score was eighteen out of twenty, which was attained by table number eight. Just behind them was table number eleven, with seventeen out of twenty, and then table number nineteen, with fifteen out of twenty. Congratulations to the three prize-winning teams, and thanks to everyone for joining us this afternoon."

Her three teammates were delighted to have finished second, but Amy felt otherwise. "I'm pissed for two reasons. First, assuming the winning team's answer was Macedonia, we actually won the trivia, with eighteen correct where they had seventeen. Barry ripped us off. And second, I had promised to control myself, and I failed in that promise."

"Well," laughed Eddie, "you only promised to *try* to control yourself. And you did try, didn't you?"

Amy nodded. "That's a subtle point, and you're right. I did try. Now I can't figure out why Barry went through all that excess verbiage in his question. As Jeremy had suggested, Barry could have just asked which is the first country, alphabetically, beginning with M. Then we probably would have tied for first, and there would have been a tiebreaker question. I guess Barry is just a big fan of the Summer Olympics and he couldn't control himself, so he had to throw it into the question."

Having been looking at Eddie, Amy now smiled in Jeremy's direction, but was surprised to see that Jeremy had left the table. He soon returned with a big smile on his face.

"Where were you, Jerry?" inquired Amy.

"I was at the obvious place. I went to the winners' table—they are still there, waiting for Barry to give them their prize, as are we—and I asked them what their answer was to Question Thirteen. They said they had not even thought of Macedonia; their answer was Madagascar. So we would have come in second regardless."

Amy was disgusted. "So I made a loudmouth pest of myself for no reason whatsoever. Swell! I was too smart for my own good, and—it turns out—for no possible benefit."

Her husband smiled. "Sweetheart, again, as you like to say, you're sure as hell right about that." Laughs all around. "I guess they knew that Paramaribo is the capital of Surinam. Maybe one of them has a friend or relative from there or currently living there. What was the other impossible question? I don't even remember it."

"It was to name the two countries with the most islands," responded Eddie. "You had to correctly give both to get the point. We guessed the Philippines and Indonesia, and Barry said the answer was Norway and Sweden, each with over two hundred thousand islands, which sounded ridiculous to me. So when he said that, I checked it out on my phone, and he was correct."

They received their gift certificate from Barry and, as they walked back to the apartment building, Cathy had another question regarding the Lance Redding murder case. "Amy, couldn't the killer have been a burglar who came in through the unlocked window at, say, twelve thirty in the morning, expecting to be unobserved, and then he shot John when John confronted him? He may have previously cased the area and, therefore, he already knew that the window would likely be unlocked."

Amy was about to ask, "Who's John?" and then she realized that she had referred to Lance as John. "Yeah, Cathy, what you are suggesting is certainly a possibility. John's house is in a wealthy area and could, indeed, be the target of a burglary. Thanks for asking; I had not previously considered that possibility."

They reached the apartment building and said their goodbyes. Amy and Jeremy walked to their car, half a block away, and drove home. Cathy and Eddie got in the elevator and smiled at each other.

"Well," Cathy laughed, "again, Amy did not fail to disappoint us!"

"You bet!" replied her husband. "As Amy herself mentioned, she's sometimes too knowledgeable for her own good. And we did pretty darn well, as a team, coming in second."

"Yeah," Cathy replied. "Second place, plus a wild show by Amy—who could ask for more?" They both laughed heartily as they unlocked the door and entered their apartment.

Tuesday, October 30, 2018, Morning

At nine fifty-five, Amy walked through the main entrance of a Manhattan office building on Lexington Avenue, in the Thirties. She took the elevator up to the twenty-fourth floor and proceeded to open the door to suite 2407, the headquarters of Arno Consulting.

Amy told the receptionist that she had a ten o'clock appointment with James Berkman, and he told Amy to take a seat, after which he made a phone call. Two minutes later, a short but muscular man, whom Amy knew was thirty-eight years old, came out, smiled at Amy, and said, "Hi, Amy, I'm Jim; let's head for my office."

Amy rose, they shook hands, and then she followed Jim to a well-decorated office, where he motioned for her to sit on one end of a large sofa. Jim seated himself on the other end of the sofa. "So, Amy, George says he's retained your firm to solve Lance's murder. I certainly want to help you in any way I can, so please fire away."

Amy smiled. "Well, I wouldn't want to put it quite that way!" They both laughed. "I guess I would like you to tell me everything you can about Lance. Nothing is too unimportant to mention. In my most recent murder case, a seemingly unimportant and seemingly totally irrelevant piece of information, mentioned by someone I interviewed, proved to be critical in solving the murder."

Jim nodded. "Okay, I first met Lance in 2011, when he joined our recruitment group—I'm the group leader. He immediately proved himself to be extremely successful in getting companies to utilize our services. He had an unusual, confident personality, including periodically wearing the fox outfit he told us he wore at college as the mascot of two sports teams.

"Frankly, I have no idea of why his approach worked as well as it did. If I was deciding whether to sign up with Arno, I would expect a more subdued recruiter who quietly—but thoroughly and professionally—went through the details of Arno's expertise in helping my company succeed. I would have thought that this was far too important a decision for Lance's kind of antics.

"But clearly, I was wrong. I freely admit that. As they say, in Latin, *res ipsa loquitur*, the thing speaks for itself. We were, indeed, very lucky to have had Lance on our team."

"Jim," interrupted Amy, "can you describe the relationships that Lance may have had with women, if you are aware of any such relationships?"

He nodded. "There is only one 'relationship'—if you want to call it that—that I am aware of. Lance made a play for my girlfriend. And he knew, at the time, that she was my girlfriend."

Amy was shocked. "Oh my god, Jim; oh my god!"

"Well, Amy, it happened. In 2013, my first wife and I divorced. It was an amicable breakup; we simply realized that after seven years of marriage, our two lives had gone in different directions.

"Then in July of 2015, I met Annette. We clicked with each other immediately. Within a few weeks, we decided to become exclusive. She occasionally visited me in my office, and I introduced her to my colleagues—including Lance—as my girlfriend. In March of 2016, I asked her to marry me, and she said yes. At that time, we moved in together. Our wedding occurred in August of that same year.

"Now, going back to January of 2016, I received a phone call from Annette about an hour after she had left my office, where we had eaten box lunches together. She said that when she took the elevator down to exit the building, Lance followed her into the elevator, flashed a big smile, told her she looked fantastic, and asked her if she wanted to join him at his apartment some evening, preferably very soon.

"Annete told me that she was very surprised to have Lance come on to her like that, and she said something to him like, 'Sorry, no way; I'm with Jim.' I was more than very surprised; I was shocked and angry.

"A few minutes after receiving that phone call, I confronted Lance, and he apologized profusely. He said that for some reason he could not explain, he had lost control of himself. Lance assured me that it would never happen again, and he begged me to forgive him. So I did forgive him, and he kept his promise.

"Of course, it is overwhelmingly likely that this was not an isolated incident for Lance. I'm confident that he tried to steal lots of other men's girlfriends; I presume it gave him a big ego boost when he succeeded. Very sad. But I have no additional direct knowledge regarding Lance's relationships with any other women."

Amy changed the subject. "So, Jim, tell me about Lance's fox party."

He nodded. "Of course, Lance would have had no objection if Annete had come with me to the party, but she understandably declined. So I drove there alone, and there was Lance, outside his front door, in his fox costume—smiling fox head and all—greeting me and some other guests who arrived at the same time as I did.

"We all enjoyed the buffet, then the live music and also Lance's antics, dressed in the fox outfit. We also enjoyed some fun conversations. There was no unpleasantness whatsoever, as far as I am aware. The party ended at around nine, and—again, as far as I am aware— we all left at that time. I drove straight home, arriving at around nine forty-five, and I was home for the rest of the night. Annette will certainly confirm that."

"Jim, where do you live?"

"On East Twenty-Eighth Street, only a few blocks from here. Is there anything else you'd like to know?"

"Jim, were there any companies recruited by Lance to employ the services of Arno Consulting who have complained that Lance misled them, and they were not receiving what they were promised by Lance?"

He was contemplative for a few seconds, then he nodded his head. "As a matter of fact, yes. About a year ago, Daniel Fields, the CEO of Fields Insurance Advisors—which is basically a one-man operation—came to this very office, and he was very angry. He said he was not receiving from Arno what Lance had promised when he recruited Fields Insurance Advisors to sign up with us. He threatened to take us to court.

"At that time, Fields Insurance Advisors had been our client for about eight months. I felt that Daniel had unrealistic expectations and was also being unreasonably impatient with us, but I decided—with the agreement of my superiors—to agree to refund 75 percent of what Fields Insurance Advisors had paid us as a non-refundable yearly fee and terminate our relationship with them. That was acceptable to Daniel, but he was still a very unhappy and angry man, muttering about how Lance was a scoundrel.

"That's the only company I am aware of that has, in any way, criticized Lance for misleading them in his recruitment efforts. I had actually forgotten this incident until your question brought it back to me."

"Only one more question. Do you have any idea of who might have killed Lance? Even if it's just a gut feeling, I'd like to hear about it."

Jim smiled and nodded. "Yes, I think the killer may well be some guy whose girlfriend was recently stolen from him by Lance."

They rose, shook hands, and then Amy departed and headed for her Spy4U office, arriving at eleven thirty. She checked her messages, and then she phoned her husband and related to him what Jim had told her. "So, Jerry, what do you think?"

"Well, sweetheart, this guy Daniel Fields is certainly a suspect—but a very unlikely one. However, there may be other companies whose CEO—or other top guy—still has this festering anger at Lance for misleading them. Jim said he's not aware of any other such companies, but that doesn't mean they do not exist.

"Also, it's now totally obvious that Lance had this thing for stealing the girlfriends of friends and colleagues. Psychologically, it gave him a needed feeling of masculinity and superiority over the other men. Once he stole these women, he didn't have much use for them, and he abused them until he left them, or until they left him. Of course, this is a general pattern, and I'm not saying it held up in all cases."

"Jerry, you're sure as hell right about that. This afternoon, I'll be back at Arno Consulting to interview Madeline Davies, another Arno person who was at the party. She was the one non-member of the Balch College political discussion group who was at the tavern. And Ralph told me that she was just as knowledgeable as the other five."

Her husband was nervous. "Sweetheart, you're not gonna get into a political debate with her, are you? That would not be wise."

"No, Jerry, of course not. And, in light of our recent trivia contest, do you know the likely reason why the company was called Arno Consultants?"

"I guess because Florence, Italy, is on the Arno River, and one of the founders of the company had some sort of particular affinity for that city."

His wife had an alternative explanation. "Jerry, you may not know this, but the Arno also flows through Pisa, so the founder may have been fond of Pisa and/or Florence."

"No, I didn't know that. By the way, do you remember what you said that you later realized might have been important?"

"No, I still can't remember, and I'm very frustrated."

"Well, sweetheart, have fun with Madeline, and remember, no political squabbles!"

Amy laughed. "Will do."

Tuesday, October 30, 2018, Afternoon

Madeline Davies was already sitting in the Arno Consultants reception area when Amy arrived at three twenty-five. She rose and introduced herself to Amy, and then they headed for Madeline's office. Amy noted that Madeline was very conservatively dressed, in a pantsuit, and that she was a very beautiful woman.

Madeline took a seat at her office desk, and Amy sat facing her on the other side of the desk. The hostess initiated the conversation. "Amy, yesterday evening, I was visiting with a friend, Janice, and her husband, Larry, an NYC police detective, and I mentioned that you were coming to interview me regarding the murder of a business colleague.

"Larry told me that you were famous at the NYPD as the modern-day version of Sherlock Holmes. He said his fellow detectives refer to you as Sherlock Bell!"

Amy managed a smile. "I appreciate the compliments, but I hate that nickname. However, I'm confused. I see a lovely diamond ring on your left-hand ring finger. Doesn't that mean you're engaged to be married, or maybe even already married?"

Madeline laughed. "The ring I'm wearing is my late mother's engagement ring. I'm a single woman. But this job is fantastic; I'm very lucky to have it. I do not want to endanger it in any way. So I will not mix business with pleasure, and I don't want any man here to even think of going out with me. So I told everyone here that I'm engaged to a military man who is on a top-secret two-year deployment overseas, and therefore, I can't give his name or even show his photograph.

"I've been with Arno for six months, so, a year and a half from now, I'll have to come up with a new story." They both laughed.

"But I know you want me to tell you about Lance. Shortly after I arrived, he came into my office with a big smile on his face and said, 'Madeline, you are a beautiful, sexy woman, but don't worry. I have a strict rule to never, ever come on to a woman who is married or engaged to be married.' And he never did come on to me nor said anything which was in any way inappropriate after that.

"But strangely, what Lance said to me—plus his looks and personality—made me become, over time, more and more attracted to him. When I was invited to his fox party, I made a rash decision—I would remove the ring from my finger before I arrived, and I would leave it off throughout the duration of the party. And I would make sure that Lance got a chance to observe this.

"I know that Lance did, in fact, observe the absence of a ring, but he said nothing about it to me. And, of course, he was murdered that evening, after we left the party. But someone there did notice me—in spades—and I also noticed him!

"His name is Allen Gray, and we hit it off immediately. Allen and four other members of his college political discussion group were going to a tavern after the party to talk politics—and other things. I'm a political junkie—Allen and I had actually talked a bit of politics at the party—so Allen asked me if I wanted to join them. I said sure.

"I had a great time at the tavern, and I held my own in the political conversations. Everyone there was very respectful of the other people's opinions—I'd heard that was the big rule in that discussion group when they were at Balch College. And I had an even greater time flirting with Allen.

"At about one in the morning, we drove our cars to his house in Rego Park, Queens. I'd rather not provide any more details, but I'll just say that Allen and I are now a couple. Boy, am I happy that I removed my ring prior to the party!"

Amy nodded and smiled. "Madeline, you appear to be in your early thirties. I'm sorry if this is too personal, but how come you're still single? You are an incredibly beautiful woman!"

"I'm thirty-one years old. Ten years ago, I married my high school sweetheart. I never dated anyone else. Four years ago, Kevin died of a brain tumor. Two years ago, I started dating."

"Oh my god, Madeline, I'm so sorry. I have to ask you if you suspect—or even have a hunch—that someone in particular may have had a grudge against Lance and may have killed him?"

She shook her head. "As I mentioned, I've only been at Arno for six months; I can't give you anyone's name whom I would suspect might have killed Lance. And I would, indeed, be very surprised if the murderer turns out to be someone at Arno."

Amy smiled. "My husband told me not to do this, but I am also a political junkie. What would you say are your core political beliefs?"

Madeline burst out laughing. "Just like me, you can't control yourself!" Now Amy burst out laughing. "Amy, I'd say I'm liberal on social issues and conservative on fiscal issues. So I do not fit nicely into either party. In the 2016 election, I strongly disliked both Trump and Hillary, and I'm not gonna reveal whom I voted for—I haven't told anyone—which is why they call it a secret ballot."

Again, they both laughed, and Amy decided to quit while she was ahead. "Okay, Madeline, no problem. And thanks a bundle for opening up to me about everything." Amy decided to forgo returning to Spy4U and went straight home, where she found Jeremy doing actuarial computations on his computer. When he was done, twenty minutes later, Amy told him what Madeline had said.

Jeremy laughed. "So Lance had some scruples; he drew the line at coming on to engaged or married women! What a saint!"

Now Amy laughed. "Yeah, based on what I've heard, I'm not sure I would have expected Lance to impose such a strict prohibition on himself."

"And, sweetheart, I don't like the idea of Madeline saying she hated both candidates. I suspect she did not vote for either of them and either sat it out or voted for a third-party candidate. In other words, I suspect that she threw away her vote.

"In the general election, one should vote based on the issues, as opposed to the primaries, where personalities can be considered. I'm sure one or the other of the two hateful 2016 presidential candidates would be closer to where Madeline stands on the issues."

Amy shook her head. "Jerry, I think you are inferring much too much from what Madeline said. I doubt that she sat it out or voted for the Green Party or whoever. However, if she did, then I agree with you that she was dumb."

"Sweetheart, this is all well and good, but are we getting any useful information from Madeline—or, for that matter, from anyone so far—that can lead us to the killer?"

She shook her head. "No, Jerry, not yet. But we are getting a fuller understanding of Lance's character. Sooner or later, something big will break—at least I hope so."

"So, sweetheart, who's next on your list?"

"That would be Doris Mays. I'm meeting her tomorrow for lunch at the Lincoln Center Diner on the Upper West Side. She and her friend drove to the party together and then drove home together—or so she says."

Thursday, November 1, 2018, Early Afternoon

At twelve thirty, Amy entered the Lincoln Center Diner, and a thirty-ish redheaded woman rose from a chair in the lobby, recognized the red scarf Amy said she'd be wearing, and introduced herself.

"Hi, Amy, I'm Doris Mays. Pleasure to meet you."

They shook hands, and the hostess escorted them to a booth in the back of the diner. They put in their lunch orders, and then Doris initiated the conversation.

"Amy, I presume you want me to tell you everything I know about Lance Redding and about what transpired on the evening of Lance's party."

Amy nodded. "That is correct."

"Okay, here goes. When we were both seniors and in the political discussion group at Balch College, Lance nearly raped me."

"Oh my god, Doris! Oh my god!"

"It was on our second date, in November. I had been very attracted to Lance, and I had made not-so-subtle hints to him that I'd like to go out with him. He was a perfect gentleman on our first date, as well as a great—and funny—conversationalist. I was thinking that on date three, I would willingly be going all the way with Lance, if you know what I mean. In fact, I was excitedly looking forward to it.

"But on date two, a different Lance emerged. We were supposed to go to a movie, and as the theater was near Lance's apartment, he suggested that we stop at his apartment before the movie. He said he wanted to show me his coin collection. But there was no coin collection. Shortly after we entered the apartment, Lance started ripping off my clothes, and then he pinned me down on the rug, getting ready to do the act.

"I don't know how I did it, but I managed to escape from him, grab my handbag and some of my clothes, and run out the door. It was a terrifying experience, something totally unexpected. I managed to get home with the help of a stranger who happened to be in the elevator when I entered it to go to the ground floor and exit Lance's building.

"I did not speak to Lance after this, and he did not try to contact me—neither to apologize nor to ask for another date.

"Finally, in April, Lance approached me after our discussion group meeting to ask me a question regarding a position I had advocated in a discussion the group was having regarding the Israel-Palestine situation—our group sometimes extended our conversations to international politics. I asked him if he was going to apologize to me, and he responded that I was right; he had not carefully thought out the implications of the position he had advocated at the meeting. It was clear that Lance had no recollection whatsoever of what had transpired on our second—and final—date. That was the last time we spoke to each other until Lance's fox party."

"Doris," interrupted Amy, "did you tell any other people about what Lance did to you?"

"The only person I told was my girlfriend, Marilyn Waller, whom I brought as my guest to Lance's party. She told me she would only accompany me if I promised her not to make a big scene there. And I kept my promise.

"But I did have a brief private conversation with Lance a few minutes before Marilyn and I left the party and drove home. I was very calm and said to him, 'Lance, are you sorry about what you did to me on our second and final date when we were seniors at college?'

"Lance had a very confused look on his face and responded, 'Are you sure we went out on any dates? I don't remember anything like that.' I just walked away.

"But I do not regret at all going to the party. The food was great, the live music was great, and, best of all, I met a guy! His name is Peter Regan. He's handsome, smart, and has a good job. We've seen each other several times since the party, and I'm very optimistic!"

Amy nodded and smiled. "Doris, that's great news. So you say that after the party, you and Marilyn drove home, right?"

"Yes, I drove Marilyn to her house, where we hung out until about one in the morning, and then I returned to my house."

"Aside from what Lance did to you, have you heard any stories about Lance mistreating other women?"

"Well, about a year after we graduated, I heard some gossip about a woman who had been living with Lance and who committed suicide shortly after she broke up with him and moved out. And, later on, I heard about Lance's first and second wives, who both divorced him, claiming physical and mental abuse."

"Even if it's just a feeling, is there anyone in particular that you suspect might have killed Lance?"

Doris shook her head. "No, I wish I could help you more, but don't think I can."

Amy paid their bill and then headed back to her Spy4U office, where she phoned her husband and related what Doris had told her. "So, Jerry, Lance's party seems to have turned out to be a matchmaking service. First, Madeline, and now Doris. And also, maybe Marilyn, with Ralph."

Her husband laughed. "Don't worry, Lance was not as good a matchmaker as you are. The matches for Madeline and Doris were just luck, and besides, they may not last. Your matches have resulted in marriage. Anyhow, the more people speak to you about Lance, the worse he sounds. And we're told that before he put on the fox outfit sometime in his junior year at college, he was a quiet, unassuming guy."

"Yes, Jerry, so we're told."

"And you still don't remember what you said that you realized, later on, might be important?"

"Right, I still don't remember. Anyhow, this afternoon, at four o'clock, I have an interview at the Arno Consultants headquarters with Martin Katz, the other Arno colleague of Lance's who was at his party."

"Okay, sweetheart; again, have fun!"

Thursday, November 1, 2018, Late Afternoon

"At three fifty-five, when Amy showed up in the reception area of the Arno headquarters, a short, unattractive, very overweight man rose from his seat and greeted her.

"Hello, Amy, I'm Marty; let's head for my office."

They sat in cushioned chairs, facing each other, and Amy, glancing at a photo on the desk, had a question.

"Marty, is that a photo of you and your wife?"

"Yes, it is. My first wife married me when I was much thinner. As I gained weight, over the years, she became more and more angry. She left me six years ago, when I was thirty-two. I assumed that—looking the way I do—I would be single and lonely for the rest of my life.

"But I was wrong. I met Rita two years ago, when I was checking out at the supermarket, and she was the cashier. There was a malfunction of the cash register, and we had to wait there for several minutes until the supervisor arrived. During that period, we were talking to each other, and sparks flew for me—and, as I found out later, for her. I asked Rita if she was single. She replied in the affirmative, so I asked her for her phone number. Six months later, we got married.

"I can't imagine what a beautiful woman like Rita could have seen in me. But I am so eternally grateful that she did see something—whatever it was that she saw."

Amy nodded and smiled. "Wow, Marty, that's quite a story! Did you ask Rita to attend Lance's party with you?"

"I did ask her, but she declined to go. I had made the mistake of occasionally reporting to Rita some of the awful things that Lance had said to me about women—and, specifically, about women he had been with. Rita remembered, and she said she wouldn't want to be anywhere near Lance, ever. Then Rita told me to have a great time at the party, and while I was there, she'd continue reading the book she'd recently been enjoying.

"At the party, I talked mainly to Jim, my colleague at Arno Consultants. There was some great food at the buffet, and the live entertainment—including Lance, in his fox costume—was nice. At nine, the party ended, and I drove straight home to Rita. I know you're trying to solve Lance's murder, but that's just about all I know."

"Marty, what kind of awful things did Lance say to you about women?"

"Amy, I'm not happy repeating this stuff. Lance said women were created to obey and serve men, and to accomplish this goal with a woman, a man must speak and act in a dominant manner, with regard to the woman, during a decent percentage of the time he spends with her. He said that just like when parenting children, a certain amount of discipline is sometimes necessary, to accomplish the desired result. Stuff like that.

"With regard to a particular woman he was with, Lance would sometimes say things like how she's not up to the required level of obedience and service to him. He said that a guy must not directly demand this of a woman, but he must appropriately guide her into that proper status.

"Now, of course, I have no idea how much of that kind of talk was just bluster. But I guess I can see how Rita would be justified in refusing to go to Lance's party."

Amy was nonplussed. "Oh my god, Marty, oh my god!"

"Anyhow, Amy, that's all I know. I have no reason to suspect anyone who was at the party—or anyone else—of being the killer."

Shortly after that, the interview ended, and Amy headed for her apartment. When she arrived, she kissed her husband.

"Jerry, as you know, I secretly record all my interviews while investigating a case, and I want you to listen to my interview with Marty. If I told you what he said Lance told him, you wouldn't believe it."

Jerry performed as instructed, and when he finished listening, he appeared stunned. "I can't believe that here, in the twenty-first century, an intelligent, educated man can think that way, let alone tell a colleague about it."

Amy smiled. "Well, his reward for having that attitude was two failed marriages, and, also, possibly, getting murdered.

"Anyhow, Jerry, I think the key to this case is why kill Lance now? There are several possible answers. The first possibility is that fairly recently, Lance did some horrible thing to a woman, who then made the decision to kill him. Or maybe he recently stole a girlfriend from a guy, and the guy was angry enough to murder him. The second possibility is that the killer was someone invited to the party who decided that it would be a convenient time to kill Lance, as they would be at his house anyway, and there had not previously been a convenient time. Frankly, I find that hard to believe. Or third, the motive may be a recent event not related to Lance's behavior toward women. In any case, once we determine the motive—which must include the reason for killing Lance now—we'll probably be able to identify the killer."

"So, sweetheart, as you are rejecting possibility number two, I guess that means we haven't found a seriously plausible killer yet, right?"

She nodded. "Yeah, that's the way it currently looks to me."

Friday, November 2, 2018, Morning

At ten-thirty in the morning, Amy entered the Woodside, Queens location of Regan Insurance Brokers. She identified herself to the receptionist, and after less than a minute, a well-tanned, tall, prematurely balding man came through a door and introduced himself to Amy as Pete Regan. They shook hands, and she followed him back to his office, where they took seats. He spoke first.

"Amy, I have friends in the NYPD who say you are the absolute best there is regarding solving murders."

Amy's face turned red. "Well, I don't think I'd go that far."

He smiled. "And you're modest too! Anyhow, I know you want me to tell you everything I know, so here goes, okay?"

She nodded. "Sure, you go, guy!"

"Well, I met Lance early in our senior year at Balch College when we were both members of the political discussion group—although I only attended around half of the group meetings. But I first heard about him in the second semester of my junior year, when he decided—apparently on his own—to acquire a full-body fox costume and make himself the mascot of the Balch baseball and basketball teams."

"Peter," interrupted Amy, "where would someone get a costume like that—do you go on Amazon?"

He laughed. "No, not Amazon. I remember that some of the discussion group members asked Lance about that, and he said he bought it at Carlo's Costumes, which specializes in that kind of stuff. Lance said that a relative who had acted in Broadway shows told him about Carlo's. It's in Manhattan, and you can come in and try on the costumes before buying or renting one of them.

"In any case, after Lance made his fox debut, the story appeared in our college newspaper, and student attendance at the baseball and basketball games doubled. Lance became the most famous Balch College student ever. And, apparently, many of the women at Balch went wild about Lance.

"Please understand that everything I'm now gonna say is second- or third-hand. Not only did Lance go out with lots of different women, but he apparently was very nasty—even physically abusive—to some of them. And, after I graduated, I heard a story that he had badly mistreated his live-in girlfriend, and, shortly after she left him, she committed suicide."

"Pete, did you ever hear anything about Lance stealing other people's girlfriends?"

He nodded. "Yes, I did. Right near the end of my senior year, one of the discussion group members—I don't remember who—was very upset and blurted out to me that Lance had stolen his girlfriend. This guy told me he was sure that Lance did it just to prove he could, and to confirm that Lance was more of a man than him."

"Oh my god, Pete, that's so awful!"

He nodded. "Yeah, Amy, you're right; that is, indeed, awful. So when I received the invitation to Lance's fox party, I was not sure that I wanted to go, even though it sounded like lots of fun. But my friend Allen—whom I met when we were seniors and in the discussion group—said he'd be going, and he convinced me to go too.

"And I was lucky I did. As expected, everything—the food and live music—was great, and Lance's fox antics were cute too. But I also met a nice lady at the party; her name is Doris Mays. She was in the discussion group, but I really didn't remember her—and she didn't remember me either. We've been going out; at some point, we might even get serious!

"But Allen got even luckier. He hit it off immediately with Madeline Davies, a colleague of Lance's at Arno Consulting. I shouldn't tattle, but Allen told me he ended up getting really lucky—if you know what I mean—that same night. Now they are talking about moving in together. Allen recently told me he believes that he and Madeline will eventually get married. So Allen will be ever-grateful to Lance in heaven—or wherever Lance is currently located." Both of them laughed heartily.

"Pete, even if it's just a hunch, is there anyone in particular that you suspect may have murdered Lance?"

He shook his head. "No, and besides, we all have great alibis for the time of the murder, which I've been told was between eleven and one that evening. We were all at McCloud's Tavern, and that's for sure. McCloud's was the absolute highlight of the whole evening. We renewed the pleasure and intellectual challenges we had at the political discussion group. I now realize how much I've missed those experiences. Maybe we can get together periodically at McCloud's—or somewhere else—to have our discussions. I think I'll contact the others with that suggestion.

"I wish the other nine discussion group members had accepted Lance's party invitation. I think they would have had a great time, and they would have enjoyed the discussions at the tavern. Of course, some of them likely don't now live in this area and/or had other obligations."

Amy smiled. "With regard to alibis, not everyone at the party went to the tavern, and there may be other suspects who were not at the party."

"Yeah, Amy, of course you're right; I got carried away. But I can confidently say that there is no one at all whom I suspect—or even have a hunch—may have murdered Lance. And if I can think of any additional information about Lance, I promise to contact you."

The interview ended, they rose and shook hands, and Amy headed for Spy4U. When she got there, she checked her messages and then phoned her husband, to whom she related what Peter had told her.

"So, Jerry, any comments?"

"Sweetheart, I wonder if the guy who told Peter that Lance stole his girlfriend was Howard, the guy who told Ralph about how Lance stole his girlfriend and then abused her."

"No, Jerry, it could not have been Howard. Ralph told me that Howard graduated one semester early, and Peter's guy spoke to him near the end of their senior year. So that makes two discussion group members whose girlfriends were stolen by Lance; isn't that special?

"Anyhow, based on what Jim said, we know that right up to the present, Lance pursued other men's girlfriends. And any one of those men—particularly if there's a guy whose girlfriend Lance stole recently—could, indeed, have become enraged enough to kill him."

"Sweetheart, do you think it's possible that one of Lance's ex-wives killed him?"

"No, I think that's very unlikely, but obviously, I have to talk to them, regardless. But one thing is for sure; somebody killed him. Probably somebody he abused in some way. And both his wives claimed that Lance abused them, physically and mentally."

"So, sweetheart, who's next on the list?"

"That would be Howard Argus. He brought his sister to the party, and then he drove her home before heading for the tavern. We're meeting for dinner, at six fifteen, at Vinnie's Village Diner on West Fourth Street."

"Hey," Jeremy interrupted, "that's right near us!"

"Yeah, Howard said it would be okay if you joined us; I'll go home first, and then we can walk there."

"Sure, sweetheart, I'll come. And don't worry, I won't speak unless I'm spoken to."

"Perfect, Jeremy; that will be perfect!"

Friday, November 2, 2018, evening

Amy and Jeremy arrived at Vinnie's at five past six and relaxed on the sofa near the entrance until Howard arrived at six twenty. They made their introductions—Howard said to call him Howie—and were led to a booth, where they put in their orders for drinks and food.

Howard was of average height and somewhat overweight. Amy thought he was very good-looking, from the neck up. She initiated the conversation. "Howie, Ralph told us that you had a horrible experience with Lance stealing your girlfriend. Can you give us all the details?"

"Sure, it was, indeed, horrible. I met Joan in early December of my senior year. After a couple of great dates, we became exclusive. She was a junior, and she was smart, sexy, and lots of fun to be with. She was also from a religious Christian family with conservative values. She made that clear from the start. So I did not rush her or put any pressure on her regarding sex-related activities. I was definitely taking it very slow, but I was making some progress, if you know what I mean."

Amy smiled and nodded. "Yes, Jerry and I know what you mean." Howard laughed.

"Anyhow, one evening in January, we went to a basketball game between Balch's team and that of another college. At the game, Lance, dressed in his fox costume, performed his cheerleading antics. The crowd went wild, and Joan was laughing hysterically at Lance's antics.

"I have no idea how I could be so stupid, but I told Joan that I knew Lance, as we were both in the political discussion group, and

I asked her if she'd like to meet him. So after the game, we went to the dressing room, and I introduced Joan to Lance as my girlfriend. We were only with Lance for, maybe, three minutes, and then I took Joan home.

"Two weeks later, Joan told me she was very sorry to have to hurt me, but she was ending our relationship because she was now with Lance. I initially thought she was joking—and it would have been a totally inappropriate joke. But it was not a joke. I was physically ill for several weeks thereafter, and I missed my graduation ceremony in late January.

"Then in early March, I received a phone call from Joan; she was in tears. She said that she had made an awful mistake by leaving me for Lance, and she was begging me to take her back.

"Joan then gave me all the gory details. Lance had gotten her to violate her Christian beliefs and give in to have sex with him. It was something like their seventh date. Then she said, on their very next date, they were at his apartment when he announced that they were through, threw her up against a wall, and then dragged her out of his apartment and said he never wanted to see her again.

"I did take her back, but things were no longer the same between us, and I ended it after a few dates. She was no longer the romantic, enthusiastic, optimistic person I had loved—or, at least, liked a hell of a lot. I could understand why, but I just couldn't take it."

Amy nodded. "Yeah, I heard some of those details from Ralph; thanks for filling in the gaps. Did you ever speak to Lance again, after he stole your girlfriend?"

"No, never, at least not until we arrived at Lance's party—'we' being me and my younger sister Sarah. My wife, Dora, did not want to go to the party, but Sarah, who had heard about Lance, wanted to go as my guest; she said it was mainly to see his fox antics. After the party was over, I drove Sarah home, and then I drove to the tavern to be with the other discussion group members—except for Doris, who drove her friend home and did not go to the tavern."

"Howie, do you agree with Ralph—and some of the others too—that the tavern visit was the highlight of the evening?"

He nodded vigorously. "Absolutely, for sure! It brought back such happy memories for me, and I'm pretty sure we all felt the same way."

"Did Sarah have any comments about whether she enjoyed Lance's party?"

He smiled and nodded. "Yeah, she thanked me profusely for taking her to the party and said she had a great time. She said she tried flirting with Jim—who was not wearing a ring—but then he told her he was very happily married."

Amy changed the subject. "What kind of work do you do?"

"I'm an insurance adjuster at MetLife."

"Oh my god, Jerry is an independent actuarial consultant, and he got his start as an actuarial trainee at MetLife!"

This resulted in an extended conversation regarding insurance between Howard and Jeremy, that went on and on, and made Amy deeply regret that she had asked Howard that question.

Eventually, they ended it, and Amy had more questions. "Howie, even if it's just a gut feeling, do you have any ideas as to who may have murdered Lance?"

"Other than Joan, I have no ideas whatsoever."

"Do you have any information regarding what happened to Joan after you ended your relationship with her?"

He smiled and nodded. "As a matter of fact, yes, I do. As I understand it, she married a Methodist minister who was quite a few years older than she was. And that's all I know."

"Howie, can you tell me Joan's last name when you knew her?"

"It was Broder; unfortunately, I don't know the last name of the minister she married or where his church is located."

As usual with these restaurant interviews, Amy paid the check for all three diners. Then they said their goodbyes and Amy and Jeremy began their walk home. Amy asked her husband what he thought of the interview.

"Sweetheart, are you gonna interview Sarah?"

"Yeah, she's now on my list; why do you ask?"

Her husband shrugged his shoulders. "No reason in particular. But now we know—for what it's worth—that Jim does not wear a wedding ring. And Lance succeeded in stealing the girlfriends of at least two members of the political discussion group. As you recently said, isn't that special!"

"Jerry, why would Lance go after the girlfriends of guys that he'd be seeing frequently thereafter at the discussion group? Wouldn't that make the meetings very uncomfortable for Lance, as well as for the other guys?"

He smiled. "Well, Lance stole the two girlfriends from the two men in the discussion group right before those men were about to graduate—one in January and one in June—so problems at future group meetings would not be an issue for him. But Lance did try to steal the girlfriend of a colleague at Arno Consulting, which is even worse, as it could have seriously affected his career. So it's clear that Lance simply could not control himself.

"And, of course, Joan is a suspect, particularly if her marriage to the Methodist minister did not work out."

Amy nodded. "Yes, Joan is a suspect, but the question remains, why kill Lance now, after all these years? It seems so unlikely at this point, but I'll try to find out her current situation, and maybe speak to her."

"By the way, I guess I have to ask you if you've figured out what it was you said that you later on realized might be important?"

Amy shook her head. "No, dammit, I still cannot remember. And I'm getting more and more frustrated about it."

"Are you gonna try to speak to Daniel Fields, the guy who felt Lance misled him about Arno's services?"

She nodded. "Absolutely, I've been trying to contact him; I've left several messages. Of course, if Daniel is the killer—which, as Jim said, is very unlikely—it's very likely that he will not be willing to speak to me. I also went on social media and asked if anyone knows a person or company that feels they were misled by Lance's recruiting efforts, which got them to employ Arno's services."

"Sweetheart, that's a very smart thing to do."

She kissed him. "Well, I'm very smart! And if you're smart, as soon as we get home, you will remove all your clothes and head for our bedroom. I plan to spend a long time exploring your body before I totally satisfy you, and vice versa. And I definitely expect that vice versa part!"

Jeremy nodded and smiled; he was, indeed, smart enough to know exactly what was coming, and he had absolutely no complaints about it.

Saturday, November 3, 2018, Afternoon

Marilyn Waller had specifically requested a lunch date with Amy on a Saturday at this location, so, at twelve fifteen, Amy arrived at Panera Bread in Jackson Heights. Jeremy was playing his weekly tennis match, but Amy was pretty confident that Marilyn would not have wanted him there in any case.

Marilyn showed up five minutes later; they gave in their orders—Amy paid for everything—and took seats at a table. Marilyn immediately spoke. "Amy, I'm happy to meet with you and I want to help you solve Lance's murder, but I don't think there's anything I can contribute that you don't already know."

Amy smiled. "I've had people tell me that, and then they provided a seemingly worthless piece of information that gave me the solution to the crime. So just tell me everything you can."

"Okay, sure. I knew Lance when we were both seniors at Balch College—as was my good friend Doris—but I was not a member of the political discussion group. For most of that year, I had a boyfriend, Steve. Nice guy, but after graduation, I grew tired of him and broke it off.

"I found Lance to be very sexy and good-looking. If I had not been seeing Steve, I think I might have flirted with Lance and made it as obvious as I reasonably could that I wanted him to ask me out. I've heard that Lance came on to many women, but he never came on to me. I was lucky; Doris said she told you what Lance did to her, and I'm sure she's not the only girl at Balch College whom he sexually and/or physically assaulted.

"But, other than Doris, I did not hear any stories about Lance mistreating women until after I graduated. About a year after I graduated, there was this story being passed around that a girl moved out and left Lance after a period when they were living together, and then shortly thereafter, she killed herself."

"Marilyn," interrupted Amy, "do you think she may have been suffering from some sort of severe depression, and it might not have been Lance's fault?"

She shook her head. "That's what I first thought, but then I heard that her brother had said that during his sister's entire life, she was the exact opposite of being depressed, until she moved in with Lance. I have not actually seen any media references to the suicide, nor to the brother's comments, so I cannot be certain that any of this gossip that I heard is true."

"Do you remember the name of that woman, or maybe her brother?"

"No. Remember, that was a decade ago, and, anyhow, I'm not sure that I ever knew those names. Anyhow, during the years after that, I learned that Lance had married twice, and both women sued for divorce after less than a year of marriage, both claiming to be victims of mental and physical abuse."

"So, Marilyn, tell me about the party."

"Well, the food was great, and the live music was good. Lance, as expected, had his fox outfit on and did quite a performance. What was quite unexpected for me was that I requested and received a guy's phone number. When I first saw Ralph at the party, he seemed a bit lost, standing there with a detached look on his face. He was unusually thin, but something about him attracted me. I walked over and started a conversation while smiling and looking him in the eye. But I don't think Ralph realized that I wanted him to ask me out.

"So after about five minutes of this, I decided that it was now or never. I straight-out asked Ralph for his phone number. He looked shocked but pleased. He told me that he was in the recovery phase of an illness—he said not to worry, his doctor guaranteed him that it was not contagious—and he wanted me to wait a month to call him so that he'd have gained back some weight by the time we went out. Then he gave me his number.

"My guess is that he was ashamed of how thin he looked. Anyhow, three days from now, it'll be a month since the party, and I'll phone Ralph and see if he meant it about now going on a date. I'm actually quite excited about the prospect of phoning and then dating him!"

"Marilyn, even if it's just a gut feeling, is there anyone that you suspect may have killed Lance?"

She shook her head. "Sorry, Amy, no idea whatsoever."

They finished their food, shook hands, and exited. Jerry was back from his tennis match when Amy arrived home. Amy went over her interview with Marilyn. "Jerry, she thought she had nothing helpful to provide, but I think she was wrong."

Her husband nodded. "I guess you mean that the girl who killed herself probably did it due to her time with Lance, and not due to some sort of depression that had nothing to do with him. And you now think that the brother of the woman who killed herself is a suspect. But, as you've been saying, why now, after a decade?"

Now Amy nodded. "You're right. That's been the sixty-four-thousand-dollar question. Not only that, but we don't know her name. I would like to speak to her brother in any case if we can ever identify him."

"So, sweetheart, who's next?"

"It's dinner this evening, at six thirty, at Dunnigan's Steakhouse in Montclair, with Daniel Fields, the businessman who complained that Lance misled him. I finally got to speak to him on the phone, and he jumped at the combination of an interview and a free dinner at Dunnigan's. He said it would be no problem if you came too.

"But, Jerry, that would require that you really clean yourself up, starting with a shower and continuing from there. And you have to dress appropriately."

He laughed. "I'll come, and of course I'll do all of that stuff. I wouldn't have it any other way!" He laughed again.

Saturday, November 3, 2018, Evening

As Amy, Jeremy, and Daniel were being escorted to their table at Dunnigan's Steakhouse—following their introductions in the entrance area—Amy decided that Daniel's appearance could be characterized by three Cs, namely compact, confident, and capable. They ordered drinks, and then Daniel initiated the conversation.

"Guys—or Amy, specifically, I guess—I know what you want, namely for me to tell you all I can about Lance Redding, based on my experience with him. So that's what I'll do right now, so that we can all enjoy some great food and some fun conversation after that. Okay?" He looked at Amy, and she nodded in his direction, so he continued.

"My firm acts as insurance agents, finding clients the absolutely perfect type and amount of insurance to buy, as well as the absolutely perfect insurance company to buy the insurance from. In a sense, I am a salesman, so I am embarrassed at how I fell for Lance's sales technique.

"His incredibly infectious enthusiasm succeeded in selling me a relationship with Arno Consulting, where they did an excellent job performing services which I didn't need and a horrible job of not performing services which I actually did need.

"And Lance did know exactly which services I needed. I detailed them to him and reiterated them. So after about eight months, I traveled to Arno's Manhattan headquarters, and I personally spoke to James Berkman, the head of their recruitment group. I explained why I wanted to terminate our relationship with Arno and receive a full refund of our payment in advance for the full year. I explained how Lance knew what we needed and, instead, provided us with what we did not need.

"James spoke with the higher-ups and then came back with an offer to refund 75 percent of our money. I immediately accepted his offer; I felt that it was fair."

"Daniel," interrupted Amy, "do you know of any other companies who also had a gripe with Lance?"

He shook his head. "No, but as Lance undoubtedly puts on the same show with every potential client, there must be others that he also deceived badly. And that's all I know about Lance; I'll be happy to answer any other questions that you may have. And, by the way, I was with my wife, Flo, all evening on October 6; I understand that's when the murder occurred. Also, from eight thirty until eleven thirty, one of Flo's friends was visiting us at our home."

Amy smiled and nodded. "Daniel, I think you've covered everything. If I think of anything else during dinner, I'll bring it up, and if I think of anything after that, I hope I can contact you about it."

"Sure, Amy, no problem at all."

They enjoyed their drinks, and then their dinners—all three ordered steak—and they had some enjoyable conversations about non-controversial topics. Then as they were waiting for their desserts, Daniel asked Jeremy what he did for a living. Amy feared another protracted discussion about actuarial science, but when Jeremy told Daniel that he was an independent actuarial consultant, the only response from Daniel was that his cousin was an actuary, and based on what she told him, actuaries are very well paid. Jeremy nodded and that was the end of it.

OUTFOXED BY MURDER

After Amy paid the check, they ended the interview, shook hands, and departed for their respective homes. While driving home Amy asked her husband for his impressions. "Sweetheart, maybe I'm a naïve sucker—as Daniel says he was, with regard to Lance's enthusiastic recruitment pitch—but I'm 98 percent confident that Daniel is not the killer."

Amy laughed. "Jerry, if you're a naïve sucker, then so am I. I'm 99 percent confident that he's not the killer, and that makes me a lot more confident than you are!" They both laughed heartily.

"But, sweetheart, Daniel is almost certainly correct. There must be other companies with a gripe against Lance; we just don't know who they are."

She nodded. "I agree with you. But remember, I did put out my requests on social media to find out if someone knows of any people or companies with a gripe against Lance. So far, no responses, but we can hope."

Sunday, November 4, 2018

Amy Bell and Denise Bromfield were sitting at a table at an Upper West Side Starbucks for noontime cappuccinos and pastries.

Denise was one of Amy's best friends, which was not predestined to occur, given the way they met.

Denise was raised in poverty by a single mother and could not afford to go to college. Instead, she went to work full-time to help support her two-person family. Eventually, she landed a desirable job as a waitress in the executive cafeteria—actually a high-class sit-down restaurant—at the Connix Corporation headquarters on the East Side.

All along, starting as a teenager, Denise had been an extremely avid reader—of roughly seventy to eighty books a year. And she somehow retained a lot of what she read. Denise particularly enjoyed books on business and finance, although she read books on a wide variety of topics.

Denise had also become a very beautiful woman. One day, in early 2009, when Denise was twenty-seven years old, she served lunch to—and chatted briefly with—the CEO of Connix, who did not usually dine at the executive cafeteria. A few hours later, the CEO—who was twice Denise's age—returned to the executive cafeteria to ask Denise out to dinner that evening. Two months later, to the shock of everyone at Connix, they were married.

OUTFOXED BY MURDER

It was a generally happy marriage, but, tragically, three years later, the CEO died. Per his will, Denise was his sole heir, and she inherited a dollar amount in the low nine figures. She used some of that money to set up a charity, Return to Learn, and became its president.

Amy and Denise first met when Amy was engaged in a murder investigation. To solve the case, Amy had to unlock some of Denise's most personal—and highly embarrassing—secrets. But Denise had developed a connection with Amy—and vice versa. So all was forgiven, and they became very close friends over the ensuing years. Denise greatly respected Amy as a genius detective, and Amy viewed Denise as the smartest woman she ever met—with substantial knowledge in a wide variety of fields due to all the books she had read and learned from—despite having never gone to college.

Amy was instrumental in getting Denise together with her second husband, Gary Bromfield, a professor of Russian history at North Jersey College. Gary moved in with Denise at the spacious, luxurious Upper West Side condo where Denise had lived with her first husband.

Amy told people that Denise was incredibly lucky to have found Gary. She felt that the overwhelming majority of men would not have the self-confidence to be with a woman like Denise, who was so incredibly beautiful, so incredibly smart, and so incredibly rich. They would feel totally emasculated.

While sipping her drink, Amy asked her friend a question which always resulted in an interesting answer. "So, Denise, what fun topic are you and Gary currently discussing—or, probably, debating?"

Denise laughed. "I wouldn't exactly say debating, but we're discussing what should be the proper US reaction to the murder of Khashoggi."

Amy was perplexed. "Who the hell is Khashoggi?"

Denise smiled. "I thought you might ask me that. Jamal Khashoggi is the Saudi dissident writer who was murdered in Istanbul, on October 2, by agents of the Saudi Crown Prince. Gary says that we have to take strong action to sanction Saudi Arabia. I say we should not cut off our nose to spite our face. The last thing we want is to have Saudi Arabia look to Russia and China for friendship and support.

"Based on some books I've read, written by Middle East experts, we have to keep the Saudis on our side, as they are the critical factor in the whole area, as a counterbalance to Iran."

Amy was thinking, *Of course, you've read several books on this topic!* as Denise continued, "We cannot allow our disgust and rage at this horrible killing to sabotage our position in the Middle East, which can also hurt our other allies in that area. Amy, what do you think?"

Amy nodded, smiled, and tried to disguise her ignorance. "Yeah, I completely agree that the US should never cut off our nose to spite our face."

"So, Amy, do you have an interesting current case you can tell me about?"

"I sure do!" Amy proceeded to describe the essentials of the Lance Redding murder case. Again, as with Cathy, she called the murder victim John. "So do you have any ideas?"

Denise was contemplative for a while, then she spoke. "Here's my guess. Someone—either a woman abused by John or someone close to that woman—was so enraged that they wanted to kill John. However, being a law-abiding citizen who also did not want to risk spending decades in jail, that person refrained from taking action.

"However, recently, some major event occurred that, for some reason, affected that person so deeply that they decided that they had to kill John.

"This was not a sudden decision. First, the killer had cased John's house and discovered the unlocked window. Then they acquired an illegal gun. It was a seriously and carefully planned murder.

"Now, it's up to you to figure out what was that major event. After all, you are the superstar detective."

Amy nodded. "I really appreciate your analysis. Anything else?"

"Yes, one more thought. All these perfect alibis make me very uncomfortable. I'd feel much better if they weren't so perfect. You're missing something here, something very big."

Amy laughed. "That's the exact line I've used with Jeremy, regarding some previous tough cases. And it certainly applies here. Also, we have to get together with you guys very soon."

Denise nodded. "Absolutely! Actually, we're thinking of going on an eleven-night Christmas/New Year's Caribbean cruise. Want to join us?"

Amy nodded vigorously. "Sounds great; I'll speak to Jerry, and I'm sure he'll love the idea."

When Amy returned home, she related to him what Denise had said. "Do you agree?"

"Yes, but basically, Denise is just rephrasing what we've been asking ourselves for some time, namely, why now? I also agree that it's a bit weird that everyone seems to have a great alibi. And that cruise sounds like a great idea; let's do it!"

"Okay, I'll tell Denise that we're in."

"So, sweetheart, who's next? And whoever it is, I'm sure they also have a great alibi!" They both laughed.

"It'll be Allen Grey, who looks like one of the two big winners that evening."

"You mean him and Madeline, right?"

Amy nodded. "You bet! Based on what I heard from Peter, they'll soon be moving in together."

Monday, November 5, 2018, Morning

At eight forty-five, Amy walked into the Lexington Avenue offices of Midland Securities and told the receptionist that she had an appointment to see Allen Grey. Allen had told Amy that the time of her visit had to be such that it would definitely be over before the stock market opened for trading.

They got to Allen's small office, and he was at the door to greet Amy. Amy thought the best way to describe Allen's looks was that he was not handsome, but quite cute. He was six feet tall and on the thin side, with a well-trimmed beard and mustache. She sat opposite Allen, on the other side of his desk.

"Allen, I guess the first thing I should say to you is congratulations—if you know what I mean!"

He smiled broadly. "You mean Madeline and me, right?" Amy nodded. "Well, I'm so lucky; it's unbelievable! Within ten seconds of the time I first saw Madeline at the party, I was completely lovestruck—I don't care if it's an inappropriate word; I'll use it. She was the most beautiful woman I had ever seen. And yet, she was not wearing a ring! She was standing alone—thank God—and I immediately walked over and started a conversation.

"Later on, Madeline told me that Lance's party was the first time in a long time that she had not worn her mother's engagement ring when in the presence of one or more of her Arno colleagues. This was to do everything possible to avoid mixing business with pleasure. If she had been wearing the ring, I never would have approached her.

"After speaking with Madeline for a while, it was obvious that in addition to being beautiful, she's smart, sweet, and caring. She was very interested in US politics, so I asked her to join me, after the party, with the other four discussion group members, at McCloud's Tavern. She immediately agreed.

"We left the tavern at about one o'clock, and we both ended up at my house, where I'll let you guess what happened. And it's getting better every day."

"I have a question," interrupted Amy. "Are you a big fan of Mama Cass?"

Allen looked totally confused. "Mama who?"

Amy smiled. "Oh, I'm sorry, never mind. Please continue."

"Okay, Madeline and I are now working out the details of moving in together. And I think marriage is in the cards."

Amy smiled and nodded. "Allen, that sounds fantastic! Can you tell me everything you know about Lance, past and present?"

"Of course I can, but there's not very much to tell. I met Lance when we were both seniors and members of the Balch College political discussion group. I was quite shy when I was in college, so I generally kept a low profile in the discussion group, and I did not get to know Lance very well.

"I am aware that other members of the discussion group have heard stories of how Lance abused women. However, I, personally, had heard no such stories until Peter mentioned it to me when we were discussing being invited to Lance's party. And of course, Peter himself was reporting this stuff second or third hand.

"There's only one 'slimy' thing I do remember, from Balch College, regarding Lance. Shortly before graduating, I recall one of the guys in the discussion group—I have no idea which one; there were something like twelve men in the group—muttering that Lance had stolen his girlfriend.

"After we graduated, I did hear about Lance's two divorces, but I didn't have much interest in Lance, and therefore, I did not look into it sufficiently to know that the wives had claimed physical and mental abuse.

"At the party, everyone was friendly, and I heard nothing at all about Lance's abuse of women or about him stealing other men's girlfriends. Lance was wearing his fox costume, with the smiling fox head, and everyone laughed at and cheered his antics."

"Allen," interrupted Amy, "what would you say was the highlight of the evening—not counting Madeline?"

"Oh, no doubt about it, the tavern was the highlight. That discussion group was also the highlight of my years at Balch. I'm gonna do everything I can to set up periodic meetings of the group, for those still in this area. Maybe we can even have Zoom meetings, where everyone can participate, regardless of location. I can't figure out why I didn't think of this years ago, let alone when we were invited to the party. Ralph deserves a lot of credit for thinking of it and then making the arrangements."

"Do you have any idea—even if it's just a hunch—of who might have murdered Lance?"

He shook his head. "I wish I could tell you that I have some sort of suspicion, but I don't. I certainly hope that you will be successful in identifying the killer."

The interview ended, and Amy proceeded to Subway, where she bought a footlong tuna sandwich and brought it to her office to consume for lunch. As usual, she checked her messages and then phoned her husband to give him the update. "Any feedback, Jerry?"

"Yeah, who is this mystery discussion group member who was muttering, just prior to graduation, that Lance had stolen his girlfriend? Now we have two people who've mentioned this. I doubt that it's one of the guys from the discussion group who attended the party, because in that case, I think Allen would have recalled that it was them."

Amy nodded. "So if possible, I should obtain a list of all the political discussion group members during Lance's senior year, and then I should contact all of them who were not partygoers."

He nodded. "That's right—well, only the male club members; Allen said there were about twelve males in the club, so there would be roughly seven male non-partygoers."

"Jerry, you have a point. I'll see if there is a list of club members during Lance's senior year. I know Lance had such a list—that's how he got to invite all the group members to his party—but I don't know how to get a hold of Lance's list."

"Okay, sweetheart, who's next?"

"I have an appointment with Sarah Argus—Howard's sister—at three o'clock this afternoon. After that, I'll head for home. And I think I'll sexually dominate your body; be ready to remove your clothes and be totally submissive. You will be appropriately rewarded."

Jerry had no retort for that except to say, "Sure, okay."

Monday, November 5, 2018, Afternoon

As Amy entered Mike's gym, she had fond memories of her most recent murder case, where Mike's played a role in her investigation. She headed for the main room and, as expected, saw and approached a cute, "super-stacked"—to use a word Amy invented and often used—woman in her mid-twenties, exercising on the treadmill, wearing the promised dark green baseball cap.

"Hi Sarah, I'm Amy."

"Amy, I hope you don't mind if I stay on the treadmill while we talk. Monday is one of my two days off—I work Tuesday through Saturday at a restaurant—and on my days off, I want to do all the exercising that I can."

Amy laughed. "I can understand that; no problem. As I mentioned on the phone, I'd like you to tell me everything you know about Lance and the party."

"Sure, I never met Lance, but I had heard stories about him, so when my big brother Howie told me that he was invited to Lance's fox party, and Mona did not want to go with him, I asked him to bring me along. I promised that I would not interfere with his fun in any way.

"Of course, I planned to have my own fun. And I did, except for not finding any eligible bachelors to go out with."

"Sarah," interrupted Amy, "I take it you've never been married."

She nodded. "That is correct. Engaged twice, but they did not lead to marriage; I called both of them off. I have no trouble attracting guys, but I guess not the right kind of guys."

Amy smiled. "I can definitely see how you would attract lots of guys." They both laughed, and then Sarah continued.

"There was one good-looking guy, not wearing a ring, sitting alone, so I sat down on an empty seat next to Jim—he told me his name, and vice versa—and started a conversation. I had a great time talking—and sort of flirting—with him until he told me he was happily married.

"But I did love the party—the food, the entertainment, Lance's fox antics—and I told Howie that I was very grateful to him for taking me as his guest. Now to get to what I know about Lance—of course it's all second and third hand stuff, so I cannot vouch for any of it.

"First of all, I heard that Lance was an incredibly sexy guy. And when he put on the fox outfit, danced around, and then removed the outfit, it drove a lot of ladies wild with sexual excitement. That's why I wanted to see for myself at the party. And although I did not feel the wild excitement, I could see why some women would.

"I also heard that Lance had been physically abusive to some women, even driving one woman to suicide. In addition, as I understand it, both of his wives divorced him, claiming physical and mental abuse. But, as I said, this was all just word-of-mouth.

"Therefore, under no conditions would I have ever made a play for Lance, nor gone out with him if he asked me to. I'm not that much of a masochist. But, Amy, if you know a nice guy to introduce me to, I'd be very grateful."

"Sarah, what do you do at the restaurant where you work?"

"I'm an assistant manager. In my spare time, I exercise, and I paint—on canvas, not on walls inside houses. I've always been very interested in art."

"So who would be your favorite painter?"

She thought about it for a few seconds. "I guess that would be Monet."

"Are you into politics?"

Sarah laughed. "Actually, I'm into thinking and talking about anything I find interesting, and that would encompass lots of things, including politics, religion, and life in general."

"Do you have any additional information on the suicide, such as the name of the woman who killed herself?"

"Sorry, no; I'm pretty sure that I've told you everything I know."

Amy thanked Sarah for agreeing to speak to her, and then headed home, where she dominated Jeremy, as promised. Then when they had both recovered, she told him what Sarah had said.

"So, sweetheart, are you gonna play matchmaker again for Sarah?"

Amy smiled. "Well, I do like Sarah, so if I find a single guy whom I think fits her bill, I'll see if I can fix them up."

"And now, that makes three people who've heard about the suicide."

She nodded. "Yeah, and one of them heard about the woman's brother saying she was never depressed until she moved in with Lance. But that was a decade ago. Again, we're back to the big question, namely why now?"

He smiled. "Yeah, we always come back to that. I guess I'll ask my standard question. Have you remembered what you said that may be important?"

"No, Jerry, and I'm starting to doubt that I'll ever remember."

Tuesday, November 6, 2018, Morning

Election Day. Amy and Jeremy voted at nine fifteen, and then she headed for Spy4U. At ten thirty, there was a knock on her office door, and Chester entered.

"Hi, Amy, have you made any progress yet on the Lance Redding murder case?"

She smiled. "Nothing yet that I can brag about, but I think I'm clarifying the situation."

He laughed. "That's a great way of describing it. You may have to take a one- or two-day leave from the case, as an old friend of mine, Herb Jackson, came to me with—as you say—a situation, and I think you're the one to at least take a shot at identifying a thief.

"Herb is in my office now, and I would really appreciate it if you would accept his case. I'm only asking you to allocate no more than two days—probably just one day—to this. Of course, as usual in these kinds of cases, it'll be your decision as to whether to accept the case. Are you free to join us right now, in my office?"

Amy knew that this meant she had to accept the case, and she had to proceed immediately to Chester's office. That was totally obvious from the way Chester presented it to her.

She smiled and nodded. "Sure, Mr. Murray, I can go to your office right now."

When they arrived, a man who appeared to be in his mid-fifties rose and shook her hand. He was about five foot seven and in good physical shape, with a big, clearly visible bald spot on his head.

"Hi, Amy—Chester said we should use first names—I'm Herb." They all took their seats on comfortable, cushioned chairs, and Herb spoke.

"Amy, I don't know if Chester told you this, but he and I were good friends while in college. Then we graduated, and I set up my business in Atlanta, while Chester moved to New York City. Still, we kept in contact, and we got together every two or three years.

"About three months ago, business developments had reached a point that clearly required me to move my business to New York City—Jamaica, Queens, to be exact—which was, in many ways, a major hassle. Of course, there was one great benefit, namely that Chester was here, in New York City.

"Five of my employees were able to move here with me; four of them had been with me for several years, and the other one, Bernard Stokes, joined my firm six months ago. He is a very talented employee, and, sadly, I think the other four don't like him because he sometimes may overshadow them.

"Bernard tries really hard to be a friend to the other four, and I keep hoping they'll fully accept him. I've made subtle suggestions to that effect.

"Anyhow, Bernard has an interesting background. He was an English major at Georgia State University. And then he received a full fellowship to get his master's degree at Zeus University in Athens, Greece, in a bilingual, English/Greek program. Bernard's mother is from Greece, and Bernard told me that he speaks pretty good Greek.

"While studying in Athens, Bernard won some sort of literature contest at Zeus University, and the prize was a first edition of a book written shortly after Shakespeare died, critically analyzing some of his plays. If you opened the front cover—which had a modern plastic cover over it for protection from the elements—you would see a certificate, attached to the first page via a paper clip, bearing the same message, in both English and Greek. In English, it reads, 'Bernard Stokes, winner, First Prize, Literature Challenge, Zeus University, Athens, Greece.' And it also gives the date.

"Bernard cherished that book, and he often brought it to work and sat at his desk, eating a sandwich for lunch while rereading sections of the book. But he did not want to aggravate the obvious jealousy of his colleagues, so he said to me that he never told any of them that he got his master's degree in Athens, Greece, at Zeus University, nor that he spoke Greek, nor that the book was a valuable first edition.

"Anyhow, last Wednesday, at ten past noon, I called Bernard into my office—when he was reading his book while he was eating lunch at his desk—as a problem had arisen that required his immediate attention. The other four were planning to leave at twelve thirty for lunch together at a local restaurant. The five of them all had desks in the same large room.

"Our conference in my office ended at twelve forty, at which point Bernard returned to his desk, and the sandwich—actually the half that was uneaten—was still there on his desk, but the book was gone.

"Other than Bernard's four colleagues, there was a secretary there while we were in my office, until she left at twenty-five past twelve, and there was also a cleaning woman there for part of the time. But I'm 99 percent sure that one of Bernard's four colleagues stole his book, basically out of spite."

"I spoke to all four of them, and they all said they were sympathetic with Bernard's frustration about his book being missing, and there must be some reasonable explanation for what happened to the book. They all said that they wanted to help Bernard to locate his book. They also told me that they would be happy to speak to any investigator that I might hire, and that they're all free for interviews this afternoon, as well as tomorrow afternoon—Chester told me that you can only devote at most two days to the investigation. Amy, I hope you will agree to take on the case."

Amy pretended to be spending a few seconds in deep thought, deciding, and then she nodded. "Yes, Herb, I accept the case." Chester smiled broadly at Amy and displayed a thumbs-up as Amy continued. "I would like to bring my husband, Jeremy—I call him Jerry—to join me at the interviews if he is available." Herb nodded in agreement. "By the way, Herb, what does your firm do?"

"The name of our firm is Jackson Services. We're involved in security; I'd rather not elaborate. But frequently, we have to meet with clients in person, and at this point in time, the majority of our clients are in New York City, while very few are in Georgia."

"So if it's convenient for you, then, as Chester had suggested, I'll set up your four interviews for this afternoon, here in his office. I have Nathan Corning at two, Brittany Lume at two thirty, Jane Kingman at three, and Albert London at three thirty. I'll tell them that Jeremy may also be there and to use first names. No need to interview Bernard; he's too traumatized right now."

Amy nodded. "That's fine with me." They rose, shook hands again, and Amy returned to her office and phoned her husband. She related what had just transpired in Chester's office. "So, Jerry, as the interviews start at two o'clock, can you be here by one thirty, just to be sure?"

"Okay, sweetheart, I'll see you in your office at one thirty."

Tuesday, November 6, 2018, Afternoon

Jeremy showed up at Amy's office at one twenty-five; they split a Diet Pepsi, and she asked what he thought about the case.

"Sweetheart, there's no doubt in my mind that one of the four colleagues did it, but I have a prediction. If these people have even a shred of decency, they will see how hurt Bernard is, and they will realize how mean and petty they've been. This incident may actually bring them closer to Bernard, and they might even allow him into their circle."

Amy was contemplative for a few seconds, and then she nodded. "You know, Jerry, it's far from guaranteed, but you might be right! And in any case, that's so smart, and now I'm so attracted to you! I can hardly control myself, but I'll have to, as Nathan Corning could arrive early for his interview. But as soon as we get home, you'll have to thoroughly satisfy me. Be ready." Jeremy smiled and nodded.

Nathan actually did arrive early, and at one fifty, Amy got a call from Chester. "Hi Amy, Nathan Corning is in my office, so you and Jeremy should come on over now and start the interview process. At this point, I'll leave my office until the four interviews have been completed. Then I'll return, and it's likely that Herb will show up too at that time."

So they left for Chester's office, introduced themselves to Nathan—who was wearing a sports jacket and tie—and then the three of them sat in the same chairs that Amy, Chester, and Herb had sat in that same morning. Amy spoke.

"Nathan, I appreciate you coming to speak to us. Tell us a bit about your background."

"Well, I grew up in the suburbs of Atlanta and went to Emory University. I majored in accounting, but after a few years in that field, I got bored and went to work for Herb at Jackson Services."

Amy nodded. "Okay, Nathan, as you know, at twelve forty last Wednesday afternoon, after Bernard came back from a half-hour conference in Herb's office, he discovered that the book on Shakespeare that he had been reading was now missing from the top of his desk. That book was very precious to Bernard, as it was the prize he had received for winning a literature contest while he was at college in Athens, getting his master's degree. I suspect that it was the only prize he ever received. Did you see anything suspicious in the office around that time, or do you have any idea at all regarding how this could have happened?"

Nathan smiled. "The college gave him a book on Shakespeare? That's pretty funny. Given their location, how about a book on Alexander the Great? Or, even better, on Melina Mercouri? Or maybe even an ancient coin with Homer's face on it that they just dug up nearby." All three of them burst into laughter. When they calmed down, Amy spoke.

"Well, it was some sort of literature competition, and Shakespeare is one of the top people in the field of literature. And also, it was a valuable first edition."

He nodded. "Yeah, you have a point. Anyhow, it's likely that Bernard did what we all do—in my case, frequently. He was holding the book, was distracted by something, and then he put down the book somewhere other than where he normally puts it. It could have been in a toilet stall, on a bathroom sink, on someone else's desk, on a chair somewhere, or virtually anywhere. At some point, somebody probably found it and did not know that it belonged to Bernard. So they probably took it home."

Amy nodded. "That's certainly possible. Is it true that some of you have not been as friendly as you should have been with Bernard since he arrived at Jackson Services?"

"Amy, that is correct, sad to say. We old-timers have to make much more of an effort to welcome him in as one of us."

They rose, shook hands, and then Nathan departed. Amy looked at her husband. "Jerry, do you have anything to say?"

"Yes, I have a question; are there actually any books on Melina Mercouri?" They both burst out laughing, then he continued. "I think Nathan has a point. We all misplace objects when we are distracted. I also do it frequently."

She nodded. "Yeah, that could have been what happened, although I doubt it. Bernard was reading while eating lunch—or at least that's what we've been told. So clearly, unless there's more to it, when Herb invited Bernard to his office, Bernard would have left the book on his desk. But maybe there is more to it, and he did not give Herb the straight story."

At two thirty, Brittany Lume showed up. She was petite, with red hair and freckles. Again, they took the three seats, and Amy spoke.

"Brittany, thanks for coming; are you a Georgia native?"

She nodded. "Yes, I'm from Augusta, and I also graduated from Augusta University. I majored in psychology. But you needed advanced degrees—which I did not want to pursue—in order to get a good job in that field, so after two jobs that just didn't do it for me, I joined Jackson Services. I've been here for four and a half years.

Now, if I can just find the perfect guy!" Everyone laughed, then Amy spoke.

"Okay, Brittany, as you know, at twelve forty last Wednesday afternoon, after Bernard came back from a half-hour conference in Herb's office, he discovered that the book on Shakespeare that he had been reading was now missing from the top of his desk. That book was very precious to Bernard, as it was the prize he had received for winning a literature contest while he was at college in Athens, getting his master's degree. I suspect that it was the only prize he ever received. Did you see anything suspicious in the office around that time, or do you have any idea at all regarding how this could have happened?"

"Amy, please don't tell her I said this, but I think Anne, the company secretary and receptionist, took the book. I've seen her glancing at the book—on various days, when Bernard went somewhere and left the book on his desk—and this past Wednesday, she probably saw her opportunity and grabbed it. Then she left for lunch, with the book under her coat, before Bernard's conference ended, and she put the book in her car."

Amy nodded. "That's definitely a logical scenario. But why would Anne want that specific book enough to steal it?"

Brittany shrugged. "That's beyond my pay grade. What kind of literature contest was it? Some of my friends were English majors, and I've never heard about any kind of literature contest."

Now Amy shrugged. "To use your phrasing, that's beyond my pay grade." They both laughed. "But you can ask Bernard, and I'm sure he'll tell you what kind of college literature contest they had in Athens."

"Okay, Amy, the next time I'm in Athens, I'll check it out." Both of them laughed. "And I'll try to be nicer to Bernard; we haven't been too nice to him."

The interview ended, Brittany exited, and, again, Amy looked to her husband for feedback.

"Well, sweetheart, it was probably a very valuable book, being a first edition. But I guess Anne would have had no way of knowing that it was a first edition. I doubt very seriously that she would risk her job to steal a book on Shakespeare. It makes no sense."

At two fifty-five, Jane Kingman arrived. She was tall, thin, and wearing a pantsuit.

"So, Jane, were you born in Georgia?"

She nodded vigorously. "Absolutely, Georgia born and bred. I was born, as an only child, in Albany—that's Georgia, not New York—and I lived at home with my parents while studying business at Albany State University. And until Jackson Services moved here, to Jamaica, Queens, all my previous jobs were in Atlanta."

"Okay, Jane, as you know, at twelve forty last Wednesday afternoon, after Bernard came back from a half-hour conference in Herb's office, he discovered that the book on Shakespeare that he had been reading was now missing from the top of his desk. That book was very precious to Bernard, as it was the prize he had received for winning a literature contest while he was at college in Athens, getting his master's' degree. I suspect that it was the only prize he ever received. Did you see anything suspicious in the office around that time, or do you have any idea at all regarding how this could have happened?"

Jeremy smiled and noted that what Amy had just said was exactly the same—word for word—as what she said to the two previous interviewees. This was typical of her in this kind of multiple-interview situation.

Jane nodded. "I am pretty confident that it was the maid. Last Wednesday, she was a substitute, not our usual maid. And she might have expected to never come back again to clean our office. So she took what she could and planned to sell it for whatever she could get. Why would any of the rest of us steal a stupid book?"

Amy smiled. "Well, it was a valuable first edition."

"I didn't know that, and I doubt anyone there did, but it doesn't change the fact that I can't see anyone else—including Anne, our receptionist—stealing a book. Amy, do you know what subject Bernard majored in for his master's degree in Athens?"

"I'm pretty sure his major was some kind of literature."

Jane nodded. "So it makes sense that Bernard held the book near and dear. And given what's happened, it makes me see that we all have to be kinder to Bernard."

Jane left, and again, Amy looked at Jeremy.

"Well, my idea—that this missing book would result in his colleagues being more sympathetic to Bernard and that they would treat him better—seems to have been proven correct. All three people that you've interviewed so far have indicated this."

"Yeah, Jerry, you're sure as hell right about that."

The final colleague, Albert London, arrived at three thirty on the dot. Amy observed that he was tall, fit, handsome, and around thirty years old. Amy went through her established routine of asking Albert if he was born in Georgia.

"Yes, I'm an Atlanta boy, all the way, including Georgia State University, where I majored in art. In addition to my job at Jackson Services, I am an active amateur painter."

Amy smiled. "That's interesting. Who is your favorite painter?"

He responded immediately. "It's Van Gogh, for sure. I've even visited his museum in the Netherlands."

"Albert, what topics do you enjoy talking about?"

"Virtually any topic, as long as the conversation stays civil. I would certainly call myself a conversationalist."

"You look very fit; do you exercise?"

"As a matter of fact, yes, and I tend to enjoy exercising, but I don't do it as often as I should."

Amy smiled broadly at her husband, but she wasn't sure whether he knew the reason. "I see you're not wearing a ring; may I assume that you're single?"

He shook his head. "No wife—I never found the right woman, at least so far—and no current girlfriend. I always seem to attract the wrong women."

"Albert, after this situation has been resolved, and after I finish up with a murder case I'm currently investigating, would it be okay if I introduced you to a young lady—if I find one—with whom I think you'd hit it off? I have a reputation as an amateur matchmaker, and I have a pretty good record."

He nodded vigorously. "I would love it if you introduced me to a young lady who you think is right for me. To put it bluntly, I sure hope you do!"

"Okay, Albert, back to the current situation. As you know, at twelve forty last Wednesday afternoon, after Bernard came back from a half-hour conference in Herb's office, he discovered that the book on Shakespeare that he had been reading was now missing from the top of his desk. That book was very precious to Bernard, as it was the prize he had received for winning a literature contest while he was at college in Athens, getting his master's degree. I suspect that it was the only prize he ever received. Did you see anything suspicious in the office around that time, or do you have any idea at all regarding how this could have happened?"

"Amy, the only idea I have is that Bernard is somehow very confused, and he was actually not reading the book while eating lunch this past Wednesday. Maybe he was reading it at lunch on Monday and Tuesday of last week but not Wednesday. The book is probably somewhere at his house.

"In that case, one thing is for sure, namely that when Bernard studied in Athens for his master's degree, his field of study was not memory training." Everybody laughed. "And another thing is for sure; we all have to completely accept Bernard as one of us." And that ended the final interview.

Albert left, and Amy had a giant smile on her face. Jeremy was pleased that he could inform his wife that he had figured it out. "Sweetheart, it's Sarah, right?"

"You bet, Jerry! I think Sarah and Albert would be perfect together. But of course, I do have to wait until I'm finished with the current murder case before I can introduce them."

"So, sweetheart, does this mean you're confident that Albert did not steal Bernard's book?"

"Jerry, are you telling me you don't already know who took the book?"

He was dumbfounded. "Of course, I don't already know; none of them said anything even remotely incriminating. I was there; I was listening carefully."

Amy smiled and shook her head. "It's obvious that you were not listening carefully enough. One of them incriminated themselves—at least I'm 95 percent confident that they did. Certainly confident enough to identify that person to Herb as the very likely thief."

"Okay, sweetheart, please lay it all out for me."

"I sure will! All four of them were born and raised in Georgia. Not only that, all four went to college in Georgia. So if I tell them that for his master's degree, Bernard went to college in Athens, they would all naturally assume that I was talking about Athens, Georgia, home of the main campus of the University of Georgia. They certainly would not assume that Bernard went to Greece for his master's. Note that Bernard had not ever told them anything about where he got his master's degree, nor that he speaks Greek.

"But one of the four did assume that I was referring to Athens, Greece, not Athens, Georgia, because they stole the book and read the certificate attached to the first page. Do you recall who that was?" She observed a blank look on her husband's face. "It was Nathan, my first interviewee. He suggested that given the location, instead of a book about Shakespeare, it would have been more appropriate for the prize to be a book about Alexander the Great, or—jokingly—Melina Mercouri, or an ancient coin that they just dug up with Homer's face on it.

"Bingo! Nathan incriminated himself. I'll call Mr. Murray and tell him that he can join us in his office—as can Herb—as the interviews are over and I have identified the thief."

Chester and Herb returned at four fifteen and Amy told them how she solved the case. Chester smiled at his old friend and said, "Amy always makes it look easy, but, trust me, no one else would have identified the thief."

Herb nodded. "You know, Chester, I think you're right. Well, I felt I had to know, and now I know. But I have no idea what I'm gonna do about it."

Amy smiled. "I have a prediction that may surprise you. Actually, Jerry originally gave me the idea. I think the book will 'magically' turn up in the office tomorrow. And I think that Bernard will now be basically accepted as an equal by his four colleagues. I am certainly not anything like 100 percent confident about this, but I'm predicting it."

Herb was dumbstruck. "Wow, Amy, that's quite a prediction! Thank you so much for taking on the case. To be honest, I greatly doubted that you—or anyone else—could determine the identity of the thief. And now, you've done it, and in less than two hours!"

Amy and Jeremy enjoyed a celebratory dinner at Big Tony's Restaurant on the East Side, and then they headed home. Jeremy had a question. "Sweetheart, do you think you'll receive a cash bonus for solving the case?"

"Maybe I will, but I don't know if Chester even charged a fee to his old friend. And solving the case doesn't directly benefit Herb financially. But if Herb's firm is doing well—and as it involves some aspect of security, I think it is—Herb may be grateful enough to give me a bonus regardless. I guess I'll find out pretty soon, one way or the other.

"Oh, and there's something else; I located Joan Broder. She was the girlfriend of Howard Argus, and Lance stole her. Then he physically abused her and dumped her on the very next date after she gave in and had sex with him.

"Howard said that Joan married a minister, but it looks like she's still using the last name Broder. I'll try to phone her now." Amy went into their bedroom to make the call, and she returned five minutes later with a smile on her face.

"We're set for lunch tomorrow at the Utopia Diner in Fresh Meadows, Queens. I asked her about the minister, and she said she'd talk about him tomorrow at lunch."

Jeremy shook his head. "That does not sound good. Looks like Joan cannot catch a break."

His wife sighed. "Yeah, Jerry, you're probably right."

Wednesday, November 7, 2018, Morning

At ten thirty, Amy was at Spy4U, engaged in a great celebration. This was not due to her solving Herb's case, although she was happy about that too. The source of her overwhelming joy was the results of the previous day's elections. The Democrats had flipped the House of Representatives and secured a majority. Starting in January, Nancy Pelosi would become the new Speaker.

Never mind that the Republicans had retained control of—and had actually gained two seats in—the Senate, with fifty-three seats. Trump's vile agenda was now dead in the water! She had phoned her husband several times to gloat.

Her celebration was interrupted by her phone ringing; it was Herb. "Amy, you were right! I can't believe it! A few minutes ago, Bernard went to the men's room. When he returned, he discovered the book in a bag, on the floor, propped up against one leg of his desk. And then his colleagues came up to tell him how happy they were that he found the book. Jane actually hugged him—and she had to bend down a bit to do it.

"Amy, you are a genius, one in a hundred million!"

She laughed. "Remember, as I said, Jerry gave me the idea; he is actually the genius."

"Okay, let's compromise; you and your husband are both geniuses." Now they both burst out laughing, and then Herb continued. "I don't know if I'll ever confront Nathan and tell him I know everything. Obviously, he is contrite. I don't think there's anything to be gained."

Amy agreed. "Herb, I think you're probably right about that."

Wednesday, November 7, 2018, Afternoon

The Utopia Diner was located, not surprisingly, on Utopia Boulevard. Amy sat in the lobby, wearing her red scarf, until a woman in her early thirties, who was kinda cute—as Amy would say—with short brown hair and casually dressed, approached her and introduced herself as Joan Broder.

They were led to a booth and ordered their drinks and meals. Joan ordered two moscatos and then salmon with zucchini. Amy ordered two Coke Zeros and then a burger plus fries. Then Amy spoke.

"Joan, as I told you on the phone, I was hired to investigate the murder of Lance Redding. I'm requesting that you tell me everything you know about Lance. All I know about you is what Howard told me, which basically ends with his graduation from Balch College. Howard did also tell me that he thought you had married a Methodist minister."

She nodded. "Okay, sure. I can sum up what happened before Howie's graduation in a few words. Howie was wonderful, but Lance was exciting, and I was a stupid fool.

"It's impossible to describe the sexual excitement I felt when Lance appeared in his fox outfit and then removed it and displayed his powerful personality. I know that what I just said sounds absurd, but it was true—not only for me but, as I understand it, for many other women.

"At the time when I first met Lance—which was in January of my junior year—I had been seeing Howie for a bit more than a month. Actually, it was Howie who—stupidly—introduced me to Lance. Of course, one month is a very brief period of time, and of course, I was very young—twenty years old—but Howie was by far the most wonderful guy whom I had ever met. I was actually thinking that we would end up married.

"But in a matter of a day or two, Lance changed all that. We started dating immediately, and I initially kept it secret from Howie. But I soon realized that I had to end it with Howie, so just before he graduated, I told him the bad news. Howie took it very hard.

"My parents were—and are—very religious, and they taught me to refrain from sex before marriage. I never expected to follow in their footsteps in that regard, but I had decided not to have sex until I had been in a committed, serious relationship for about six months. This had not yet occurred in my life, so I was still a virgin.

"But after about a month, I could not control myself any longer. When we returned to his house, after a great date, I gave in and had sex with Lance. And then his behavior immediately changed.

"On our next date, during which he seemed rather cold and disinterested, we returned to Lance's house, and then he became downright violent. He threw me against a wall and dragged me out the door, shouting that we were through. I had to call a friend to take me home.

"Shortly thereafter, I contacted Howie and begged him to take me back. He did, but I was no longer the same. I was constantly depressed and incapable of showing affection. Howie had to dump me. I spent the remaining year and a half of my college career in the same state. No dating and completely traumatized. I occasionally passed Lance in the hall until he graduated, a year before me, but we never spoke again.

"Even in the years after graduating, I was not the same woman as before Lance. Finally, seven years ago, I met Harvey Baker, the minister at Ditmars Methodist Church. He was in his late forties, but I realized very quickly that despite the age difference, he was exactly the man I needed. We got married three months after we met. He helped me through my periods of depression and brought me back to optimism and to God.

"I asked him if it was okay if I did not officially change my name, although I would have no problem at the church—or elsewhere—being called Joan Baker. Harvey said no problem.

"Then a year ago, suddenly, with no prior warnings, Harvey died of a heart attack. He did leave me some money, so I'm financially okay, thank God. But Harvey brought me back to life, and I'm back to liking people, so I work as a waitress three days a week—not at this diner—and today is not one of my workdays."

"Joan, did you hear any gossip about Lance after graduation?"

"I heard about his two divorces, and then there was this girl, Sandy—at least I think that was her name, I'm not positive—who was living with Lance for a while until she left him and moved out, and then she killed herself shortly thereafter. The gossip was that she was traumatized by Lance's abuse. But the person who told me that story said it had happened several years before, shortly after I had graduated. And that's all I know."

"Joan, are you back into the dating scene yet?"

She smiled. "Yes, Amy, I had my first date two weeks ago. I am, finally, truly confident in myself as a woman."

Amy nodded. "I think that's great news!"

They enjoyed their meals, and of course, Amy picked up the tab. Then they left, and Amy drove to Spy4U. Shortly after arriving, she excitedly phoned her husband. "Jerry, Jerry, guess what! I've got her name; it's Sandy—at least Joan thinks it's Sandy."

He was confused. "Sweetheart, I don't understand; does this have something to do with the movie 'Grease?' If so, it was, indeed, Sandy, played by Olivia Newton-John."

Amy laughed. "No, silly boy, Sandy is what Joan remembered she had been told was the first name of the woman who committed suicide after living with Lance and then leaving him. No one else whom we spoke to had any idea of her first name. Maybe it will help us identify her."

"Sweetheart, isn't it possible that with her newly restored self-confidence, Joan may have finally built up the courage to go and murder Lance? That would answer your favorite question, namely why now?"

Amy paused for a few seconds to consider her husband's question. Then she responded. "Yes, that is theoretically possible, but the opposite scenario is much more likely. Finally, Joan has succeeded in not letting thoughts about Lance ruin her life. There's no way that she would bring it all back by planning and executing his murder."

Jeremy conceded. "I guess you have an excellent point there. Is there anyone else on your interview list?"

"Yes, there is. I can't locate Lance's first wife, but his second wife, Betty Moreland, has agreed to speak to me tomorrow afternoon at four thirty. Guess where."

Jeremy laughed. "I'm supposed to guess? Give me a hint. No, on second thought, I don't think I need a hint. It's at Mike's gym, right?"

"Right, Jerry, you got it! I'm meeting her in their Wellness Café."

Thursday, November 8, 2018, Afternoon

At four twenty-five, Amy arrived at Mike's Gym and immediately headed for the Wellness Café, wearing her red scarf. A woman rose from a booth and waved at Amy to join her. They made their introductions, shook hands, and Amy had only one thought regarding Betty Moreland, namely that she was an absolute knockout. Beautiful face and fantastic body.

Amy saw that Betty was sporting a very expensive-looking diamond ring on her left hand and a plain gold ring on her right hand. "Betty, do those rings mean that you're married?"

She laughed and nodded. "You bet! My husband is Richard Moreland; you may have heard of him. He runs the Moreland Fund, and they just made a multi-billion dollar offer for Cranepool Oil and Gas." Amy figured that this translated as, "We're filthy rich!"

Betty continued. "We live in a lovely large house in Jamaica Estates. But I always liked Mike's Gym, so I'm sticking with him, rather than some of the closer gyms. Anyhow, I wouldn't wish that anyone be murdered, but I'm not crying about that happening to Lance. How can I help you? Actually, first, let's get some drinks."

Betty ordered a hot chocolate; Amy asked for a Diet Pepsi. Then Amy explained why she asked for the meeting. "Betty, I'd like you to tell me everything you know about Lance. No exaggerating, but no understating either. Just the facts, ma'am." They both laughed.

"Okay, Amy, here goes. A friend introduced me to Lance about five years ago, shortly after my first divorce became final. He impressed me as handsome and confident. Lance told me about his role as the Fox, in college and, occasionally, after graduation. We agreed that he would pick me up the next Saturday evening for a movie and then a snack at a diner.

"Lance told me that he'd park his car in my driveway and then change to his fox costume, so that when I opened my door, he'd be wearing the costume. And that's what happened. Then he went back to his car, changed back to regular clothes, and reentered my house. For some reason that I can't explain, that fox stuff, plus his confident way of speaking and his sexy looks, caused me to become wild with sexual excitement. I said something like, 'Let's forget the movie and head straight to my bedroom; then we'll go out for a snack.'

"We were married a few months later. Within a few weeks, Lance changed completely. He told me he was the boss, and I was supposed to follow his orders, as well as other things like that. A few months later, he started slapping me in the face when I said something he felt was 'disrespectful.' After nine months of marriage, I sued for divorce. When I claimed physical and mental abuse, that was not an exaggeration.

"When I told him that I was having divorce papers prepared, he was very apologetic and said he'd change his ways. But I told Lance that it was too late. I immediately moved out, and I never spoke to him again, except through my lawyer."

"So, Betty, how did you meet your current husband?"

"Believe it or not, it was right here, at this gym. Richard was not a member, but on that day, two years ago, he was the guest of a member. I was exercising on the treadmill, and Richard came right up and approached me. I guess I looked pretty good, at least to him." They both laughed.

"We had immediate chemistry, and Richard proposed two months later. Our engagement lasted only six weeks; then we got married. He has always maintained that while he originally came over to me because I was a very attractive woman, he fell in love with me because of my personality.

"Before I met Richard, I had two failed marriages, and I had decided that my being attractive was likely a disadvantage, as I generally attracted the wrong kind of men. I actually believed that it would be better for everyone if single people into the dating scene had to wear a full-body costume and a mask, so their interfaces with singles of the opposite sex would be based on character and personality, rather than on looks and physical attributes."

Amy laughed. "You mean something like the Muslim burka, right? But it would be worn by single men as well as single women."

"Yes, Amy. A burka-type garment would certainly fit the bill. Then at some point—maybe after the second date—the costumes and masks would be removed, so that the singles would see what their dating partner looked like. Needless to say, some people would be unhappy with what they saw and terminate the relationship, but others would stay together, where, without the original disguises, they never would have even had a first date.

"Obviously, I was always aware that this was all just fantasy on my part. But then, Richard never would have approached me if my looks had not appealed to him. And he is the most fantastic man I've ever known. So my fantasy was not even a good idea."

Amy smiled. "Well, congratulations on finally finding the right man!" Then Amy suddenly looked like she had just seen a ghost. She turned silent and put her hands over her head. Betty was worried. "Amy, are you okay?"

Amy broke her silence. "Oh my god, Betty, oh my god! I think you just gave me the information that I've been seeking for some time. You may turn out to be responsible for me solving the murder. I can't explain now, but thank you so much!

"I've got to get home and speak to my husband about this. I think he'll be as excited as I am. I'm sorry, but I have to leave now." A very confused Betty shook Amy's hand and watched her run out of the Wellness Café.

Thursday, November 8, 2018, Evening

Amy arrived home at five past six, kissed her husband, and immediately shouted out, "Jerry, Jerry! Finally, I remember! Betty gave it to me in our interview, without realizing it."

"Sweetheart, are you saying that you now remember what you said that you later realized could be important in solving the Lance Redding murder case?"

"Yes, with Betty's help, I now remember what I said! And I think I may know who committed the murder, although it's just an educated guess, and I won't tell you, at this point, who it is.

"Now, back to what I said. It was when I spoke to you after I finished my interview with Bill and Jean Santori. We were discussing the scenario where some woman—not at the party—who was physically abused by Lance might have returned later that evening, after the party was over, and killed Lance. I said that maybe she came to the house wearing some sort of disguise, so that when she showed up on the surveillance video, her true identity could not be determined."

Her husband nodded. "Yes, I do remember you saying that, but how does that help us solve Lance's murder?"

She smiled. "I'll lay it all out for you. We believed that the six partygoers who were at the tavern had perfect alibis, as they were there between eleven and one o'clock that evening when the murder must have occurred. The medical examiner had said that the murder occurred between eight and one that evening, but the surveillance video showed Lance, dressed in his fox costume, with a smiling fox head, outside his front door at around eleven o'clock. Therefore, the murder occurred between eleven and one.

"But we were wrong. The murder could have occurred at any time after the party ended."

He was confused. "How can you say that? Is the surveillance video a phony? Was it somehow tampered with?"

"No, Jerry, no tampering. But the person in the fox costume might not have been Lance! Just as an abused woman wearing a mask could not be identified, someone wearing that fox costume also could not be identified. It could have been Lance, or it could have been anyone else whose height was roughly the same as Lance—or maybe even a different height, if no one thought to compare heights. And I'm very confident that it was not Lance who went out the front door at eleven o'clock."

"Sweetheart, you seem to be saying that someone, wearing a fox costume, entered Lance's house at, say, ten fifty, through the unlocked side window and shot Lance. Then they opened the front door, briefly frolicked around, and then reentered the house and finally exited through the unlocked side window. Am I correct?"

She smiled. "You are correct, except for one key point. That person did not kill Lance. If they wanted to kill him, why go through that fox-outfit rigamarole? When they originally entered through the window, Lance was already dead, having been shot something like an hour and a half earlier.

"That person in the fox costume was the killer's accomplice—an accessory after the fact. Their sole purpose was to give someone who was at the tavern—who had just killed Lance—a perfect alibi. The killer left the party, hung around in their car until no one else but Lance was in the house, and then entered via the side den window—which the killer had opened during the party, without being observed—shot Lance, exited by the same window, and finally drove off and showed up at the tavern at around ten fifteen, the scheduled meeting time.

"Now, Howard drove his sister home right after the party, so he would have had to then drive back to Great Neck, kill Lance, and then drive to the tavern and arrive reasonably close to ten fifteen. Maybe he could have accomplished that, but, as I said, I think I know—although without any solid evidence yet—which one of the six is the killer, and it's not Howard.

"So which one of the remaining five do you think shot him?"

"Jerry, I'll tell you at some point, but not now. What we have to do now is find out, from Carlo's Costumes, who has recently bought or rented a fox costume. Even if it were feasible for the killer's accomplice to remove Lance's fox costume from his dead body, wear it to frolic outside the front door, and then put it back on Lance, that costume was bloodstained due to the shooting. Lance's other fox costumes were under lock and key, and the accomplice certainly wasn't gonna hunt for the key. So the accomplice had to have secured their own fox costume.

"Peter told me that Lance had told him and several other discussion group members that he got his fox outfit at Carlo's Costumes, which is in Manhattan." She punched in some stuff on her iPhone. "Yeah, there they are, on West Twenty-First Street, near the West Side Highway. After I originally spoke with Detective Livingston, he provided me with a 'To whom it may concern' document for me to show, saying that I'm working with the police on an important investigation and requesting that the recipient assist me in any way they can. It also provides his police contact information if they want to confirm it."

Her husband nodded. "I get it. The guy in the fox outfit outside Lance's front door at eleven in the evening probably rented his costume at Carlo's because the actual killer, who was a discussion group member—unless it's Madeline, and I'm pretty sure it isn't—heard Lance say he acquired his fox outfit at Carlo's, and the killer told this to his accomplice."

"You got it, Jerry. So if we're lucky, Carlo's can identify the killer's accomplice."

Friday, November 9, 2018, Morning

At ten fifteen, Amy entered the warehouse headquarters of Carlo's Costumes. She showed the police document to the salesman who approached her and asked to speak to the manager.

After a minute or two, a fiftyish woman approached Amy and identified herself as Margaret Sloane, the manager. Amy explained the situation, and Margaret said she'd first have to phone the Manhasset Precinct to confirm the document. With that done, Margaret asked Amy how she could assist in the investigation.

"Thank you so much for agreeing to help. We need to know if, at any time in recent months, someone rented—or possibly bought—a full-body fox costume, including a smiling fox head."

Margaret headed for the computer and punched in some data. Amy heard noise from a printer. Margaret reached down and pulled out a sheet of paper. "There's been only one rental, and no sales. The rental was for two weeks, starting on October first. I've printed out the name, address, and phone number of the customer. It's all printed out here." She handed the sheet to Amy.

Once more, Amy profusely thanked Margaret and left for Spy4U, where she phoned her husband. "Jerry, Jerry! It took me only about fifteen minutes at Carlo's to get the information. Their manager was completely cooperative. The name of the accomplice is Thomas Greener. He did a two-week fox-costume rental, starting on October first. I have his address and phone number. I'm now gonna check him out on the internet."

"Wow, sweetheart! Looks like you've identified the accessory! It's amazing; one throwaway comment, by you, that you couldn't remember for days, and another throwaway comment, by Betty, actually may have solved the case."

"Yeah, Jerry, it is amazing, but it's not yet time for a victory party. Not by a long shot."

At eleven forty-five, Amy called back. "Jerry, Jerry! I found everything! Thomas Greener is married, with two young children. And guess the name of Thomas Greener's sister—Cindy Greener! Cindy, Sandy; Joan's memory was off by one vowel. And, also, guess what! Cindy Greener died, by suicide, nine years ago. Bingo! I have an appointment to see Thomas at his office at three forty-five this afternoon. He thinks I'm looking to buy insurance."

"Wow again, sweetheart, actually double-wow! That should be one hell of an interview; you've got him dead to rights. Do you think he'll tell you whom he was the murder accessory for—in other words, the actual killer?"

"No, Jerry, I'm pretty sure he won't. In fact, he may not tell me anything at all."

"And you still won't tell me which one of the six tavern-goers you strongly suspect is the killer?"

"Not yet. But I'll tell you this. My suspect was the most instrumental person in creating this tavern alibi. Without my suspect, they all would never have had their phony alibi. Also, I think I may know the answer to the question of why now? And, believe it or not, I think I can get this suspect to confess."

DAVID SCHWINGER

"Sweetheart, you're kidding, right?"

"No, Jerry, I'm not kidding; I'm deadly serious—to use a double entendre."

Friday, November 9, 2018, Afternoon

At three thirty, the receptionist at the Flushing, Queens, offices of Lifetime Insurance Brokers ushered Amy into a small private office, where she took a seat facing the desk. The nameplate on the desk read, "Thomas Greener, Vice President, Lifetime Insurance Brokers." Five minutes later, a five-foot-ten man, in his mid-thirties and in good physical shape, entered the office.

"Hello, Ms. Bell, I'm Thomas Greener." He took his seat at the head of the desk.

Amy was immediately taken aback by the large bandages completely covering both of his hands. Thomas saw her staring and explained, "I had a terrible burn accident in September. The bandages have to stay on for another two weeks. So how can I help you?"

"Mr. Greener, I'm sorry to have deceived you"—she handed him her card—"but I'm working with the police to investigate the murder of Lance Redding." The look on his face changed noticeably. "You are an accessory after the fact. If you don't come clean, you'll probably be sent to jail for a long time. I'm really sorry about Cindy, but I am requesting that you tell me the whole story now. Please understand that the police will be checking all your phone calls and texts, and your emails. And, most importantly, please think about your wife and about your children's welfare for the next ten or more years."

Thomas had his head down, covered by his bandaged hands. Then he looked up and stared directly into Amy's eyes. "I read about the murder; Lance was shot. As you can see, there is no way that I could have shot Lance in early October. I have nothing more to say; please leave now."

Amy departed and headed home. She gave her husband an update. "Thomas's hands were all bandaged up due to burns, so, in any case, he can prove that he could not have pulled the trigger, but that won't help him avoid an accessory charge."

"Sweetheart, how come the police did not notice the bandages in the surveillance video? Then they would surely have realized that the person in the costume was not Lance."

She nodded. "That's a good question. The answer is that the long sleeves of his fox costume hid the bandages from the surveillance video. As Bill explained to me, there were several varieties of fox costumes—all of which Lance possessed in his locked closet—with varied sleeve lengths. Presumably, Thomas rented the costume which had very long sleeves, which would totally hide his hands."

"Do you think you've scared Thomas sufficiently to have him go to the authorities and turn in the killer in exchange for a plea deal?"

"I don't know. That could, indeed, happen, but I wouldn't bet on it."

"So, sweetheart, what are you gonna do now?"

"Well, I'm going on social media again; the first time I tried social media, regarding companies with a grudge against Lance, resulted in nothing. This time, I'll ask if anyone knows who was Cindy Greener's boyfriend—possibly a Balch College senior—before she moved in with Lance. Can you figure out why I'm doing that?"

Jeremy was contemplative for a few seconds, then he smiled. "Yes, I think I know why. Two discussion group members told you they heard another, unidentified group member muttering, just before graduation, that Lance had stolen his girlfriend."

Amy nodded. "Yeah, Jerry, you got it."

"And you still won't reveal who you think is the killer?"

"Come on, Jerry, you should be able to figure it out. It's pretty damned obvious. But if I get no responses on social media by tomorrow evening, I'll give you the killer's name."

Saturday, November 10, 2018, Afternoon

At two fifteen, when Jeremy returned from his tennis match, Amy had a big smile on her face. "I got one message on social media, and it locks up the case. We now know for sure who killed Lance, and it confirms what I had thought. Here's the message; it's from a woman named Rochelle." Amy had already printed it out, and she read from that sheet.

"I was a good friend of Cindy's. She was going out for about a month with a Balch senior named Ralph—I don't know his last name. She told me he was wonderful, but then she met Lance, and he completely swept her off her feet. She dumped Ralph and moved in with Lance. After that, she periodically told me that Lance was mistreating her and that leaving Ralph was the biggest mistake of her life. But, for some reason, she stayed with Lance and suffered for eleven months; then she left him. But Lance had totally destroyed Cindy's soul, and one day, a few weeks after she moved out, she called and told me she couldn't bear to live anymore. Then she hung up, and a few hours later, she was found, dead."

"Wow, sweetheart, so Ralph murdered Lance because Lance stole his girlfriend, Cindy—who he thinks may have been the one, and he never found another after that—and then Lance treated Cindy so badly that it resulted in her committing suicide. How did you strongly suspect, early on, that Ralph was the killer?"

She smiled. "Because, by his own proud admission, Ralph suggested the idea that they all should meet at the tavern—and not right after the party ended, but at ten fifteen, to give Ralph sufficient time to murder Lance and still get to the tavern on time."

Jeremy nodded. "So, sweetheart, what's the answer to the big question, namely why now?"

"When I first saw Ralph, he looked very thin, almost gaunt. He told me that he was in the recovery stage from an illness, and he told Marilyn that he would try to gain some weight. But I think that Ralph is dying, probably from some sort of cancer. He has probably been told that he has only a short time left to live.

"So he is no longer afraid of being sent to prison—although he would much prefer that he not be identified as the killer. He had always wanted to kill Lance for what Lance had done to Cindy—and maybe also to his own chance to find true love—and now, after the diagnosis of terminal cancer, there was virtually no downside for him.

"Ralph contacted Thomas, who agreed to Ralph's plan. Given that he was now incapable of firing a pistol, it was perfect for Thomas, as he could prove his innocence if he ever became a murder suspect.

"And it went perfectly for them. Thomas rented the fox costume, Ralph unlocked the den window while at the party, and, later on, at something like nine thirty, after all the guests had left, he entered through the unlocked window, murdered Lance, left through the same window, and got to the tavern by ten fifteen. At eleven, Thomas entered through the unlocked window, did his dance outside the front door, and exited through the same window. Mission accomplished.

"I'm pretty sure they both thought they got away with it. But they haven't."

Jeremy nodded. "Of course, Ralph may not have terminal cancer; you're just making an educated guess."

Now Amy nodded. "That's right, but it's a very educated guess. I'm gonna contact Ralph and see if he'll meet with me for a second time. I think I can convince him to confess to the murder, to save Thomas's ass—and Thomas has a wife, and he has kids whom Ralph would be saving from possibly losing their father for many years."

Amy went into their bedroom to phone Ralph, and she returned a few minutes later with the news. "Well, Jerry, it's all gonna hit the fan this evening. Ralph agreed to meet me at the same place as previously, Nico's Village Diner, for dinner, at six fifteen this evening. Ralph has been so friendly and cooperative; I think he is basically a very decent man. I feel very guilty about all of this. But Ralph did murder Lance."

"Sweetheart, do you want me there with you?"

She shook her head. "No, this is something I have to do alone—just me and Ralph."

Saturday, November 10, 2018, Evening

Ralph and Amy were sitting at the same table, at Nico's Village Diner, that they had been sitting at for breakfast the last time they met for an interview. They put in their food and drink orders, and then Ralph spoke.

"Amy, I received a phone call from an old friend named Thomas yesterday evening, and from what he said, you think you know everything. So tell me what you think you know."

Amy nodded. "Yes, as of earlier today, I actually do know everything. I know that Lance stole your girlfriend, Cindy Greener, who was Thomas's younger sister and may have been the most wonderful girl you ever knew. I know that after eleven months living with Lance and being physically and mentally abused by him, Cindy left Lance, moved out, and then, a few weeks later, committed suicide. You were employed in Chicago, and you may not have found out about the suicide until sometime later.

"I know that you and Thomas decided on a plan to get away with murdering Lance after the other guests at the party had left. You set up a tavern meeting to create an alibi for the time of the killing. I know that you climbed through the unlocked den window—which you had unlocked at the party—and murdered Lance at roughly nine thirty or so. I know that at around eleven, Thomas came in through the same window and, dressed in a fox costume that he had rented, he put on a show outside the front door, to give you a phony alibi.

"I also know that Thomas will be charged with being an accessory after the fact. He can claim that he didn't know you would shoot Lance and that you had originally told him that it was just a prank, but no one will believe him. He'll be sent to jail for, maybe, ten years, leaving his wife without her husband and his children without a father. That's what I know."

Ralph did not look happy. He was biting his lip and fidgeting. "Is there anything else?"

"Well, I currently do not know this for sure, but I strongly suspect that you are in the late stage of a terminal illness, which caused you to finally decide to take deadly action against Lance, as you were no longer worried about going to jail."

Now, Ralph was in tears. "You're right about everything you said, and I mean everything. I have terminal cancer, and they say I have less than six months to live—probably a lot less.

"Lance destroyed the only decent chance I had for love, and then he essentially murdered Cindy. Who knows how many other lives he ruined, and—more importantly—who knows how many more lives he would have destroyed in the future if I had not killed him. Have you told the police about Thomas yet?"

"No, I haven't." Now, Amy decided to lie. "But this coming Wednesday, I have a meeting in Manhasset with the detective handling the case."

"Okay, I'll go to the police on Monday or Tuesday and confess, if you promise me that you won't tell them about Thomas. I'll say I don't know the name or any other information about the individual whom I hired to do the fox act at Lance's house at eleven o'clock after the party. I'll say that in any case, I told that person that it was a prank, and I did not tell them that I planned to murder Lance.

"Also, the den is near the front door, and the dining room is near the rear of Lance's house, so I can say that it's likely that they never even saw Lance's dead body."

Amy nodded. "I agree to your proposal. If you confess in the manner you have described, I will never reveal Thomas's role in the murder. You can certainly tell this to Thomas. By the way, did you go out yet with Marilyn?"

"Yes, we went to dinner together yesterday evening, even though I had not gained back any weight; in fact, I had lost a few pounds. Maybe it was my last date ever. It's a shame; Marilyn is both smart and sweet."

"Okay, Ralph, let's just try, as best we can, to enjoy the meal."

He nodded. "Fine with me."

As soon as Amy left the restaurant, she phoned Chester to tell him everything. "So I expect Ralph to confess on Monday or Tuesday, and if so, I will protect Thomas. And I'm sorry I had to phone you like this on a Saturday evening. Anyhow, the Lance Redding murder case is now completely solved."

"Amy, no need to apologize. It was right for you to call when you did, and I'm very glad you called. You're saying that Betty's comment about her fantasy that singles into the dating scene should wear masks—or even burkas—is what solved the case for you, right?"

She smiled. "Actually, yes!"

"That's absolutely amazing. Also, I have some news for you. I did not charge Herb any fee for us helping him to identify the book thief. But Herb has given you a thank-you gift of four thousand dollars—I'm holding his check right here in my left hand."

"Oh my god, Mr. Murray, oh my god!"

"Well, Amy, you certainly deserve it."

When Amy got home, she provided her husband with all the happy details. "So Ralph will confess, and I get four thousand dollars! I think Herb was grateful to me for identifying the thief, but even more grateful that somehow, due to my investigation, Bernard's four colleagues are starting to accept him."

"So, sweetheart, you're saying Ralph will confess to protect Thomas and his family. Even if he's gonna die soon, that's pretty noble of Ralph."

She nodded. "Yeah, but, as I said, Ralph has always been basically a good man. Circumstances caused him to do this one bad thing. So his confessing to save Thomas is probably in line with his true character.

"I left a phone message for Detective Livingston, saying that I have identified the murderer, and I expect this person to come forward this coming Monday or Tuesday and confess."

He laughed. "Sweetheart, the detective will be in an absolute state of shock when he hears that message."

Amy smiled. "I think you're right. And Jerry, can you guess the two people that I will phone tomorrow morning—maybe actually early afternoon—regarding the same topic?

He laughed. "I know you well enough to correctly answer that question. Now that the case is solved, you're gonna call Sarah and Albert, the pair that you want to fix up. I assume you'll see if they want to go on a double date with us so that they might feel more comfortable and so that you can see how they get along with each other."

His wife nodded. "Jerry, you're sure as hell right about that."

Sunday, November 11, 2018, Afternoon

At twelve fifteen, Amy was having lunch at home with her husband when her phone rang. It was George Canfield, her client in the Lance Redding murder case. She put on the speaker.

"Amy, I just received a call from Chester. He said you've solved the case, but I shouldn't tell anyone, as the killer will probably confess in the next couple of days. Is Chester correct? That sounds too good to be true!"

"Yes, George, it's true. The case is completely solved. Obviously, I cannot guarantee that the killer will confess, but I am pretty confident that it will happen. If, however, the killer decides not to confess, then the police will try to get the necessary evidence—which they do not yet have—to charge this person with murder.

"However, confession or no confession, that individual definitely killed Lance. Hopefully, the confession will occur tomorrow or Tuesday, and then I can lay it all out for you. Otherwise, I'll have to wait a bit longer to give you all the details."

"Okay, I'll wait along with you and see what happens. Amy, as Chester originally told me, you are downright unbelievable!"

Amy hung up, and Jeremy had a question. "Sweetheart, if Ralph confesses as planned, are you gonna tell George about Thomas?"

She shook her head. "No, I won't. You and Mr. Murray will be the only people who know Thomas's identity and his motive and role in the murder as an accessory after the fact. That's my deal with Ralph. And now for my promised phone call." She punched in the number and put on the speaker.

"Hi Sarah, this is Amy Bell."

"Oh, hi Amy, guess where I am."

"Mike's Gym?"

"Yep, I just finished an hour and a half on the treadmill, and I'm sipping a fruit drink in the Wellness Café. Do you have some additional questions to ask me?"

"No, but there's a single guy I'd like to introduce to you, maybe on a dinner double date with me and my husband, or, if you prefer, without us." They both laughed.

"Amy, this is unbelievable! We just met only six days ago, and you already have a man you want to fix me up with. Wow! Yes, of course I want to meet him, and would dinner next Saturday be okay for a double date?"

"I'll have to contact Albert—that's his first name—and make sure he's available. Do you have a favorite restaurant you'd like to suggest?"

"Amy, how about the Sterling Steakhouse in Forest Hills, on Queens Boulevard?"

"No problem, I'll speak to Albert and get back to you."

They got off the phone and Amy smiled at Jeremy. "Well, one down, one to go." She punched in Albert's number. "Hi Albert, this is Amy Bell. Are you free this coming Saturday for a dinner double date with me and my husband? I want to introduce you to a great girl named Sarah. Sarah suggested the Sterling Steakhouse in Forest Hills, and she's looking forward to meeting you."

He laughed, "Holy crap, Amy, you work fast! Yes, I am available, and I'm really looking forward to it.

"By the way, on Friday, Herb called all four of us together in his office, while Bernard was seeing a client. Herb told us that the person who took the book—and then returned it—came to him, confessed, and said that they were very remorseful, so that ended it."

"Well, Albert, that's very good news."

Amy got off and called back Sarah to confirm the double date.

After she ended that call, she smiled at her husband. "So, Jerry, it's all set for the Sterling Steakhouse, this coming Saturday, at six thirty."

"Sweetheart, that's great! Do you think that one—or maybe even both—of them will come to the double date wearing a mask?" They both broke out into laughter.

Tuesday, November 13, 2018, Afternoon

At four fifteen, at her Spy4U office, Amy received a phone call; it was Detective Livingston.

"Amy, I don't know how you pulled this off—and I know it was all you—but Ralph Kane came to us at nine thirty this morning, and he confessed to the murder of Lance Redding, just as you had predicted would occur. He explained how he pulled it off, including the second person, in a fox suit, showing up outside Lance's front door at eleven in the evening to fake Ralph's alibi.

"Ralph showed us the medical reports to prove that he has late-stage terminal cancer and that he will probably be dead pretty soon. Also, Ralph will be out on bail soon.

"After acting fast to secure a search warrant, we went to Ralph's house and found the glove with the missing fibers that we recovered at Lance's den window.

"Lord only knows how you pulled this off—and I know you'll never tell me—but from now on I really should call you Super Sherlock." They both laughed. "Thank you so much for your tremendous assistance to us in this case."

"Charles, it was my great pleasure, and I greatly benefited from your presentation of the case when I came to your office."

Amy got off and phoned her husband. "Jerry, Jerry! It's all over; Ralph confessed. Detective Livingston just called me with the news. He also told me that Ralph will soon be out on bail."

"Great! So now, I presume, you'll meet with George and give him the whole story, except for Thomas."

"Yeah, whenever George wants to come in. And we can also tell Sarah—when we see her on Saturday—that the case is solved."

Saturday, November 17, 2018, Evening

The Sterling Steakhouse was an upscale restaurant, with fancy linens on the tables and servers in formal wear. Amy decided that Sarah suggested this place because she figured, correctly, that Amy would pay the check for all four of them.

They met in the reception area, and Amy could see that Albert was immediately drawn to Sarah's fantastic figure and cute face. He kept staring at her—up and down—and Sarah, who clearly observed all of this, smiled broadly as they headed for their booth.

They ordered drinks, and Amy spoke up. "Albert, as I recall, you said you were an art major in college, right?"

That was the last thing that Amy got to say for fifteen minutes. Sarah's face immediately lit up, and she and Albert began a comprehensive discussion about nineteenth-century art. Amy noted that now, it was Sarah staring intently at her date's face.

Finally, there was a break in their conversation, and Sarah had a question. "Amy, are you making progress regarding Lance's murder?"

Amy smiled. "As a matter of fact, Sarah, the case is completely solved, and the killer has confessed."

"Wow! Who was the killer?"

"Sarah, I hope you'll understand that I can't discuss anything about the case at this point, but if you check on the internet, I think you may get the information you want."

Now, Albert had a question. "Jeremy, are you also a detective?"

"No, I'm an independent insurance actuary, but I sometimes assist Amy with her difficult cases." Unsurprisingly, neither Albert nor Sarah showed any interest in what an actuary does.

The conversation—entirely between the fixed-up couple—continued on various topics, such as exercise, health in general, and whether Georgia would be in play in the coming 2020 presidential election. It terminated when the steaks arrived. Amy decided her steak was so delicious that the exorbitant price may, indeed, be justified. The others looked like they were also greatly enjoying their meals.

Sarah abstained from ordering dessert, but the other three indulged themselves. Amy could not help but observe that the fixed-up pair were continually staring at each other.

As Amy figured had been expected, she graciously insisted that she would pay the entire four-person check. No one complained. When they said their good-byes, Amy smiled broadly at her husband. "It looks like they really hit it off!"

Jeremy nodded. "I agree, possibly another big matchmaking success. And, as you just took in a four-thousand-dollar bonus, I certainly could not complain about you covering the whole check." They both laughed. "Also, I know that Ralph is a murderer, but I feel so sorry for him. Ralph got shafted—by a very bad man—in his search for love, which he never found. And now, terminal cancer at a very early age."

Now Amy nodded. "I'm with you on that. By the way, if Ralph lives longer than he currently expects to live—maybe even a lot longer—then I think that, at the trial, Ralph's lawyer should suggest that he plead not guilty due to temporary insanity. Then he should put on witnesses to detail what Lance did to Cindy—and to so many others—and how the invitation to Lance's party triggered the temporary insanity. Then the jury may decide to nullify and find Ralph not guilty."

He nodded. "I suggest that at some point, we discuss this strategy with Ralph and his attorney."

"You bet, Jerry! And, changing the subject, do you think Georgia actually is in play for the 2020 presidential election?"

"Well, sweetheart, Georgia has become, in recent years, more urban, and the percentage of whites is falling. So I think Georgia is definitely in play for 2020. I'm sure that the DNC will allocate a lot of money to Georgia to support their presidential candidate."

"Oh my god, Jerry, in their Georgia discussion at dinner, neither Sarah nor Albert said anything as smart as what you just said! How did you get so smart?"

"Well, Amy, you were truly the smart one; you married me!"

The End

About the Author

David Schwinger is retired, having spent his entire career teaching mathematics at City College, City University of New York. He now lives in Florida with his wife, Sherryl, whom he met when she was his student.

In addition to having written seventeen Amy Bell murder mysteries, David composes songs and plays trivia and pickleball. He and Sherryl have traveled to over 130 countries. David began his mystery-writing career in 2013, upon the urging of his wife.

The Teacher's Pet Murders, his first book, was inspired by the secret romantic relationship David had with Sherryl while she was his student at City College. In that book, his vivacious and brilliant heroine/detective, Amy Bell, made her first appearance. Amy has continued to use her extraordinary talents to solve murders in all of David's succeeding books.

Printed in the USA
CPSIA information can be obtained
at www.ICGtesting.com
CBHW031324191024
16129CB00007BA/215